MEET THE FOLKS OF
PARADISE CREEK, MARYLAND

Clay Mitchell: The bossy sheriff with the heart of gold runs his beloved town a little too by-the-book. He could really use some help with his love life, as well....

Uncle Albert: Clay's beloved old uncle beams with pride whenever he sees his nephew. But lately Albert's had something—or someone—else to smile about!

Lettie Rowley: This feisty, funny grandmother is looking for someone to take care of *her* for a change. Does she have her eye on someone special?

Ruth Owens and Mabel Farley: What will happen when the queens of the Paradise Creek gossip mill decide to play matchmaker? No one in town is safe from their scheming!

Hope "Red" Stevens: This runaway bride blows into town and is soon spreading joy to everyone she meets. But can her breezy ways win over the stubborn sheriff?

Dear Reader,

Welcome to another wonderful month at Harlequin American Romance. You'll notice our covers have a brand-new look, but rest assured that we still have the editorial you know and love just inside.

What a lineup we have for you, as reader favorite Muriel Jensen helps us celebrate our 20th Anniversary with her latest release. *That Summer in Maine* is a beautiful tale of a woman who gets an unexpected second chance at love and family with the last man she imagines. And author Sharon Swan pens the fourth title in our ongoing series MILLIONAIRE, MONTANA. You won't believe what motivates ever-feuding neighbors Dev and Amanda to take a hasty trip to the altar in *Four-Karat Fiancée*.

Speaking of weddings, we have two other tales of marriage this month. Darlene Scalera pens the story of a jilted bride on the hunt for her disappearing groom in *May the Best Man Wed*. (Hint: the bride may just be falling for her husband-to-be's brother.) Dianne Castell's *High-Tide Bride* has a runaway bride hiding out in a small town where her attraction to the local sheriff is rising just as fast as the flooding river.

So sit back and enjoy our lovely new look and the always-quality novels we have to offer you this—and every—month at Harlequin American Romance.

Best Wishes,

Melissa Jeglinski
Associate Senior Editor
Harlequin American Romance

HIGH-TIDE BRIDE
Dianne Castell

TORONTO • NEW YORK • LONDON
AMSTERDAM • PARIS • SYDNEY • HAMBURG
STOCKHOLM • ATHENS • TOKYO • MILAN • MADRID
PRAGUE • WARSAW • BUDAPEST • AUCKLAND

To my husband, David, who taught me to love the river.
And to the Ohio River towns of Ripley, New Richmond,
Augusta and Higginsport, where floods and friendship
are a way of life.

ISBN 0-373-16968-X

HIGH-TIDE BRIDE

Copyright © 2003 by Dianne Kruetzkamp.

Visit us at www.eHarlequin.com

Printed in U.S.A.

ABOUT THE AUTHOR

Dianne Castell fell in love with the romance genre fifteen years ago when she picked up an old Harlequin romance at a garage sale, figuring any book that looked so well-read had to be good. And it was! In fact, it was great! She was hooked on Harlequin romances to the point where she simply had to write one of her own.

Dianne lives with her husband and four kids in Cincinnati, Ohio. When not writing humorous romances, she reads them, watches funny movies, changes kitty litter—which isn't funny at all—sails and collects antique rocking chairs.

Books by Dianne Castell

HARLEQUIN AMERICAN ROMANCE

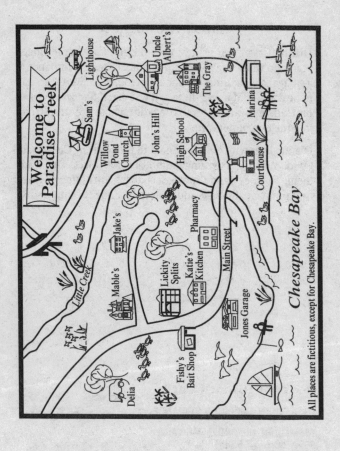

Welcome to Paradise Creek

Little Creek

Sam's

Willow Pond Church

Jake's

Mable's

Lickity Splits

Katie's Kitchen

Delia

Fishy's Bait Shop

Jones Garage

Main Street

Pharmacy

John's Hill

High School

Courthouse

Lighthouse

Uncle Albert's

The Gray

Marina

Chesapeake Bay

All places are fictitious, except for Chesapeake Bay.

Chapter One

With a siren wailing behind her delivery van and her voluminous wedding dress tangled in the steering wheel, Hope Stevens thankfully-not-Sinclare hit the brakes and swerved to avoid the geese sunbathing in the middle of the road. The screech of tires mixed with the frantic honking as a blur of gray and black swooped into the sky over the Chesapeake Bay.

The van polished off a road sign, splintered through a fence, then crunched to a stop against a huge ash tree. Air whooshed from Hope's lungs, but she was safe as an egg wrapped in cotton, protected by a wedding dress that could cover the entire state of Maryland. At least the blasted thing had been good for something after all!

"Dammit, lady!" a voice roared outside the van. "Where in the hell do you think you're going?" There was swiping at the billowing clouds of silk. "Anybody in there?"

"My name is not Dammit Lady." Did she really

say that? After twenty-nine years of being good-old, go-with-the-flow Hope who never raised her voice above polite conversation?

"What in the hell are you doing with a parachute in there?"

The material parted and she came face-to-face with a sheriff. Least she guessed that's what he was since he had a silver star, tan uniform, *what-have-you-done?* expression…and incredible blue eyes that completely took her breath away.

"Are you trying to get yourself killed? You were speeding like a madman."

"Woman." Her heart skipped a beat. "I'm a woman."

The sheriff brought his face to within two inches of hers. "The speed limit here is thirty, and it's not going to change whether you're a woman or Daffy Duck."

Surly bastard. What a waste of blue eyes. "I've driven to Dover enough times to know the speed limit on 301 is fifty, so—"

"This isn't 301." The sheriff's lips thinned and his eyes narrowed. "You missed the turnoff. This is the way to Paradise Creek and *you* are a menace to the road."

A breeze ruffled his brown, sun-streaked hair. He had terrific shoulders and was strong and fit from a life spent outdoors. If there was a pin-up calendar for sheriffs, he'd get the cover…if he ditched the *look-what-you've-done* expression.

"Now get your license, registration and your fanny out of that van."

"Van?"

His left brow arched. "The wrecked thing you're sitting in? Are you hurt?"

She had to quit obsessing over this guy. So he was incredibly handsome. Her almost-husband was handsome and look what happened there. As of today she spit on handsome. "I'm fine. Wonderful." She shook a handful of dress in his face. "But does this look like the kind of getup that has a place for a license? And there is no registration because the van's not mine. I sort of…well…borrowed it—" she stuck her head out the window so as to see the lettering on the side "—from Delia's, Catering Your Every Need."

He folded his arms across his broad chest, his brow narrowing a bit more. "Define borrowed."

"I intend to reimburse Delia for mileage." Hope eyed the crumpled fender. "And damages. I was desperate!"

"Out!"

She seethed, probably for the first time in her life. "I've had enough of arrogant men telling me what to do. In fact, I just left two grand pooh-bahs of arrogance, my ex-fiancé and my father, standing on the church steps and I have no intention of putting up with another. That means you." She fought the dress.

"And I can't...find...the blasted...handle to get out of here if I wanted to."

The sheriff yanked on the door from the outside. "It's stuck. Your dress is probably wedged in the latch. Where did you get that...thing?"

"I didn't." She pushed against the door with her shoulder. "The pooh-bahs did."

The door flung open and she gasped as skirts and slips sprang free, throwing her off balance and toppling her headfirst out of the van.

"Dang!" The sheriff made a grab for her, snagging her around the waist. They staggered, then tumbled to the ground, her on top, him below and both buried under yards and yards of expensive raw silk. He shoved material aside and glared. She sighed, suddenly tired to the bone. "I'm going to write a book, *The Wedding Day From Hell*."

"Who are you?"

"I think that might be the root of my whole problem. I don't actually know exactly who I am."

"Well, you're in luck, because we're both going to find out when you call someone to bring your license and insurance and phone Darla about her van."

His mouth was inches from hers, other parts of his very fine anatomy much closer. But with all the material between them the sheriff might as well have been a mattress as a man. Pity. But there was nothing between his lips and hers, and right now he had superb lips. They were firm and determined with a thin scar across the upper one and little crinkles at the corners. The sheriff did a lot of smiling, though right now that was only a theory. Probably some kissing. Lips like his were made for kissing. She had a sudden urge to research the kissing part.

Get a grip. Kissing an overbearing man was not part of her getaway plan. It was part of her never-again plan. "I'm not phoning anyone."

She rolled to the side and sat in the grass. "And Darla's not going to care two hoots in Hades about this van because it's Delia's."

The sheriff stood and offered his hand, pulling her to her feet, making little shivers dance up her arm. He glanced at *her* ringless left hand. "The man you left at the altar must be really worried. You should let him know you're okay, and while you're at it tell him to bring your license."

"Worried? You've got to be kidding." She kicked the grass. "The only thing that lying, two-faced, double-crossing cretin is worried about is his political career and saving his politically-correct behind. I didn't even know there was a political career till minutes before walking down the aisle. I thought he was content being a corporate lawyer until I found his campaign button attached to my bouquet between the sweetheart roses and forget-me-nots." She clenched her fists. "If there's one person I will never forget… I grabbed the button, realized my father knew about this all along since his endorsement was on the bottom, stuck my engagement ring to the bouquet and took off. I was nothing more than a political pawn!''

"If you don't want to marry this guy, fine with me. Tell him to take a hike. But do it *after* he brings your license. You've got a mess here.''

She knitted her eyebrows into a deep frown and fixed her hand on her hips, hoping to add some stern to her words. Stern was foreign territory, but she was making inroads. "In case you haven't put this all together, I'm already in the middle of a mess. Today is my day for messes. I intend to walk to the next town, get a car and go to Dover where I can sort this out and live on my own without any belligerent male interference. I'm sure my father will reimburse Delia— it's the least he can do after what he nearly did to me—and I'll send you a check for the fence and sign. I'd consider it a huge favor if you forgot you ever saw me.''

He eyed the van and her dress, then rolled his eyes so far back in his head she was sure he'd fall over.

"Just try. Okay?'' She turned for the road, dragging armfuls of dress over the grass and weeds.

"You're stressed out, Red. You're in no condition to drive. You'll hurt yourself and someone else.''

She gritted her teeth and kept on walking. "Red's my hair color, it is *not* my name. I hate the name Red, and *I am not stressed!*''

His footsteps crunched the grass behind her. "You

aren't going anywhere.'' His voice was deep and authoritative as his hand closed over her shoulder.

She clenched her teeth. ''I am *not* staying here.'' A flash of independence shot through her like a lightning bolt. ''A lifetime of marching to everyone else's drummer is over.''

She turned and pushed the sheriff right in the middle of his broad, bossy, egotistical, overbearing chest. He stumbled back, tripped in a tangle of weeds and landed flat on his backside. Her gaze fused with his angry one. ''Uh-oh.''

She spun around and ran like the devil himself was after her.

CLAY MITCHELL couldn't believe that the crazy woman in the parachute-like wedding dress pushed him, that he fell on his ass, and that she had the greenest eyes, most incredible red hair and the loveliest skin he'd ever laid eyes on. But beauty…even this much beauty…was no substitute for rationale. She was completely out of control, and she couldn't run worth a damn in that dress.

In three long strides he caught up with her, turned her around and tossed her over his shoulder.

''What do you think you're doing?''

With a soft swish, white material cascaded over his head, surrounding him like an exotic waterfall.

''Put me down right now.''

He swiped material back from his face. Afraid his

grip would slip, he clamped his arm tighter around her knees.

"Police brutality!"

"Do I look like the police?" She was slight, more dress than woman, though her fists pounding him on the back right now didn't feel so slight.

"Bully! Brute!"

"Brute's a new one. Never been called that before." She kicked the air as he headed for his cruiser. She had great ankles, nice calves. Forget ankles and calves, this was business. He opened the back door of the cruiser and dumped Red ass over appetite onto the seat. Her eyes—her big green eyes that reminded him of fine brandy sipped by the fire on a cold winter's night—were not businesslike at all. She stared up at him in disbelief as the silk settled in around her.

"What are you doing?"

"Calling Jones Garage to get that van towed and taking you to jail. And you're not getting out till you calm down."

"I am calm! Perfectly calm!" She made to get out of the cruiser but he stuffed the rest of her dress inside and stopped her dead. He slammed the door, then got into the driver's side, fired the engine and headed for town.

"You can't do this to me!" Red rattled the grating that separated the front seat from the back. "Let me out of here."

"I suggest you close your mouth and sit back and

decide who you're going to call to come get you when we reach Paradise Creek. You're not going anywhere by yourself because you might hurt yourself or someone in my town, and I take very good care of my town."

"You are the most thick-headed man on planet earth. Try and understand that *I'm running away*. That means I'm leaving you and your town. You won't have a thing to worry about. I'll go far, far away. And since I don't want to be found, I'm not calling anyone. That would defeat the whole purpose of running away. Do you see my logic here?"

"The same logic you used to justify stealing a catering van?"

"I borrowed that van!"

"You're a spoiled brat used to getting what you want. I know because my ex was just like you, full of glitz and glamour."

"I am not full of glitz or glamour, nor am I pampered. But you got me on the spoiled part." She let out a deep breath. You're making this day even worse than it is. Don't you understand this was supposed to be a great day, the happiest day of my life? Instead, I realized my fiancé was marrying me for political connections. I'm nothing but a campaign contribution, a paid-for political announcement."

He felt sorry for Red. "Betrayal's a bitter pill to swallow."

"Is that chitchat or are you speaking from experience?"

"My wife ran off to D.C. with a rich stockbroker."

"Sorry. So, do you really have a jail?"

"One with black iron bars." He watched the Open sign in the Something's Fishy bait shop flip to Closed and waved to Carlie Lewis, who was locking up the drugstore.

"That's horrible. You can't put me in there."

"Driving without a license. Grand-theft auto."

"No one in our family has been behind bars *ever*, except for a great uncle who did rum-running during Prohibition."

"You'll be carrying on a family tradition." There was already a crowd at Lickity Splits, and the aroma of crab cakes from Katie's Kitchen swamped the cruiser and tortured his empty stomach.

"How can you do this to me? You are a despicable man, void of any charm or class."

"Sounds like something my ex would say. Woe is me." He parked in front of the white clapboard courthouse in the center of town just as the bell in the tower tolled 6:00 p.m. He turned and stared at the woman in the back of his cruiser. Never in all his twenty years of living in Paradise Creek did he think he'd be locking up a bride, a really beautiful bride with hair as vibrant as a Chesapeake sunset, eyes a man could get lost in and the driving skills of Larry, Curly and Moe.

"Here's the deal," he said. "You can either walk nice and peaceful-like into that courthouse and into my office, or I'm going to carry you over my shoulder like before. What's it going to be?"

"You're just like my father and rotten fiancé—make that ex-rotten fiancé—pretentious and self-serving."

"Well, I give it my best shot."

She pursed her lips—her very sensual lips—and tried to straighten her dress, which by now really did look more like a parachute than fancy wedding duds. It sagged from her shoulders and drooped in the front, exposing beautiful creamy skin, the kind of skin men dream about. Suddenly he was feeling very much like a man.

Damn! He needed therapy—falling-for-the-wrong-kind-of-woman therapy. Since that wasn't going to happen tonight, he'd let his deputy watch her, and tomorrow convince her to get someone to pick her up. Not just for her own good, but for his, too. No alluring little body or tempting silky hair and skin to drive him nuts. Until then he'd just concentrate on her smart-ass mouth and think of her as the menace of Paradise Creek.

"I'll walk into your office, Sheriff, but I'm not, repeat not, not, not calling anyone to come get me till I have time to figure out my own life. I have no idea how long that will take, so you might as well let me go on my way."

"The D.C. police will know who you are. They'll check missing-persons, stolen vans, defunct weddings."

"My father is the master of discretion. You don't have a chance."

Terrific. "Have it your way, but we'll see how you feel about going back to D.C. after a night in the Paradise Creek jail."

THE NEXT MORNING Clay grabbed a bag of breadcrumbs from the front seat of his cruiser and slammed the door closed behind him. From the side of the courthouse he watched Herons dive into the Bay, hunting breakfast, and sailboats bobbing on their moorings. Just like any other day. Ha!

He scattered the crumbs to the gulls. How could he have locked up a woman on her wedding day and not even learned her name? Worse still, he hadn't slept worth a damn thinking about her fresh, wholesome beauty and the fire in her eyes. He liked the fire. Liked it a lot. And that was trouble. He and Red were from two different worlds with no bridge between them. Paradise Creek wasn't D.C., and he was sheriff of a small town, not a powerful politician or rich businessman.

Clay stuffed the empty bag in his pocket and entered the courthouse. He stomped down the hall to his office and went in. The heat of the potbelly stove chased away the morning chill as he tossed his hat onto the wood rack in the corner and called, "'Morning, Jake,'" to his deputy.

"'Morning,'" Jake said, today sounding younger than his forty years.

"Good morning, Sheriff Mitchell," came a familiar voice that belonged in his jail, the one with big black bars, and nowhere near his office.

He stopped dead in his tracks and turned. Red and Jake were sitting at Jake's desk, drinking coffee, eating fresh jelly doughnuts from Katie's Kitchen—looked like strawberry—and studying some magazine. He never would have imagined Red, who probably drank high tea with her pinky extended, to hit it off with beer and nuts Jake.

"What the hell's she doing here?"

Red's hair was a frenzy of soft fresh curls tumbling around her face. She had on one of the flannel shirts that Jake kept on hand in case he got caught pulling a double shift. It was opened at the throat, sleeves rolled, tails tied in the front. She looked like a fashion plate. How'd she look so good—make that terrific—in an old blue and red flannel shirt? One of those rich-people secrets.

Jake looked up and ran his hand through his black hair, that for once looked as if it hadn't been trimmed with a weedwacker. He nodded at Red. "Clay, you brought her here. Locked her up." He hitched his chin toward the oak door that separated the main office from the storage room and two jails cells. "Don't you remember?"

Clay swallowed a growl. "I mean, what's she doing in my office and not in the jail where I put her?"

Red looked his way. Her face was clean and bright, her green eyes shining. A poster girl for healthy living. She'd had a good night's sleep while he... *Damnation!*

"Jake let me out on bail, which was extremely nice of him. He's a true gentleman—" she narrowed her sophisticated brow just a bit "—unlike *some* people, and he understands that I am not a threat to society."

"You drive like a lunatic."

"It was a bad day."

"What's this about bail? And Jake's my deputy, not a gentleman."

Red smiled sweetly, too sweetly. "*Some* men can be law enforcement officers *and* gentlemen."

"I'm just a sheriff."

Jake said, "She cut my hair for bail, Clay. I lent her some clothes because she couldn't cut hair in a wedding dress, now, could she. My shirt looks pretty darn good on her, but the jeans are too big. She slept on the couch." Jake nodded across the room. "Jail's kind of dingy."

Clay groused, "It's supposed to be that way. It's jail."

"We both got hungry for some breakfast. Got to

feed the prisoners, Clay, and she even likes strawberry jelly—''

''Prisoner, hell!'' This was not the rotten night Clay had planned to persuade Red to get out of Paradise Creek. ''In case you've forgotten, bail is where someone puts up money as a guarantee the person won't leave town.''

Jake stroked his chin. ''Red's not aiming to go anywhere. Even helped me bring in some firewood. The way I see it, this was a different kind of bail. Sort of a 'get out of jail for doing some work' bail, since she hasn't any money.''

Clay turned his attention to Red. ''What happened to getting to Dover? I'll take you there.''

''See, you are a gentleman after all.''

''Gentleman has nothing to do with it. Turning my town upside down does.''

''Jake's been telling me all about Paradise Creek. The people, the events, the surrounding area. It sounds like a wonderful place. There's no reason why I can't just stay right here for a while and figure out what to do with my father and fiancé and the rest of my life.''

Clay's hormones kicked into overdrive. He did not want this forbidden-fruit, trouble-in-the-making woman distracting him at every turn.

Jake continued, ''She's helping me pick out new clothes from this here Bean catalogue I got in the mail. Your uncle talked me into getting up my nerve and asking Carlie Lewis for a date next Saturday. I want to look real good.'' He turned the catalogue around and pointed. ''I'm going to get this Atlantic-blue sweater to bring out the blue in my eyes and khaki pants to show off my lean physique, and—''

''Physique?'' Since when did Jake have a physique?

''And the classic loafer. Red thinks the classic loafer is always a good choice and I'd look dashing in—''

''Dashing?''

''Yeah, dashing.'' Jake blushed to the roots of his receding hairline, but there was a defensive edge in his voice that Clay couldn't remember hearing before. ''She said Carlie would appreciate it if I looked dashing when I took her out. That girls like it when you did things just for them and treated them special, isn't that right?'' Jake looked to Red who smiled back and nodded in agreement.

Did she have to smile? A smile like that could melt any man into a testosterone blob at twenty yards. He swiped his hand across his forehead. Potbelly stove must be working overtime. ''This is not Bloomingdale's or a boutique or a styling salon or romance central.''

Jake said, ''You all right, Clay? You're acting real strange.''

''Why don't you shove off. Get some sleep. You need it.'' *We both need it.*

Clay watched Jake leave, then turned to Red, the flip of the magazine pages and logs crackling in the stove the only sounds. He focused on the jelly doughnuts instead of the woman. The woman was far more of a temptation than any doughnut, that was for damn sure. "What do you think you're doing?"

"Helping Jake improve his wardrobe and build up his self-confidence." Red closed the magazine and looked up at him. "There's nothing wrong with that, but you sure went over the top complaining about it."

"You're making him into something he's not." He looked at her. Bad idea. Her eyes darkened to the color of warm earth. Her lips were full, ripe, natural, incredibly inviting. He felt his breath catch.

"Jake needs a boost of self-confidence. New clothes that make him feel good about himself can help and a few kind words go a long way."

She smiled again. Would he ever be immune to that smile?

"He's really got a thing for Carlie."

"Carlie needs to like Jake for who he is, not some fancy clothes and…"

"Being a gentleman? That is what you were going to say, isn't it? Of course she has to like Jake for the man he is. But clothes and manners are like the wrappings on a wonderful present. Like you."

"Like me what?"

"Your uniform is just window dressing. You'll always be the sheriff of Paradise Creek no matter what you wear. You'll always be telling people what to do and where to go and not caring if they like it or not. You are who you are.''

"And I have no intention of changing.''

"Oh, I believe you. Everybody in town believes you. But the way people present themselves can make things more interesting. Even you don't wear a uniform all the time. Besides, clothes are fun.''

"My ex had enough clothes to start her own store, and I can tell you that it wasn't fun, it was just plain expensive.''

"Jake had a budget and we stuck to it.''

He braced himself on the desk and leaned over her. "You might be able to sweet-talk him to letting you out of jail but I—''

"That place you locked me in last night is not a jail.''

Her eyes flashed like sun reflecting off the water as she pushed herself from the chair and planted her face inches from his. Her breath felt warm, even seductive, falling across his lips. She hitched her chin toward the side door that separated the main office from the cells.

"It's a disgusting dump. There are bugs. I hate bugs. I intend to write the board of…something and have you inspected so you better get it fixed up.''

Not taking his gaze from hers, he shoved the phone across the desk. "This isn't the Hilton. Why don't you call some gentleman to take you back to your cushy life in D.C.?''

He put on his sheriff face—the one guaranteed to get the results he wanted—until he realized Red smelled…familiar. His expression faltered. He inhaled again. She smelled very familiar. She smelled like…him! *She'd used his shampoo.* The kind he kept in the office in case *he* pulled a double shift. Her scent was…intimate, as if they'd spent time together, close together.

Every muscle in his body went rock hard. How could one woman cause him so many problems in so little time? ''You're getting to be a real pest, you know that?'' *In more ways than she could ever imagine.*

''Well, I give it my best shot.''

He clenched his teeth in pure male frustration. Then he backed away from her and casually made his way to the computer on the next desk. He stood behind it, hiding his present hormonal condition. He hadn't needed to do anything like this since…since never.

How could she anger him and turn him on all at the same time? He prided himself on his control but when Red was around his control was zilch. *No matter what it took he had to get her out of Paradise Creek!*

''You can't roam the streets. You're a vagrant. And if you don't call someone to come get you I will.

Runaway brides don't just vanish without anyone taking notice.''

"I'm not calling.''

"Then you're going back to jail, Red. And you're staying there till you come to your senses and make that call or someone figures out where you are and sends a limo to take you back where you came from.''

Chapter Two

Hope sat on the end of a lumpy cot and watched Sheriff Clay Mitchell yank open the door to the cell he'd locked her into a half hour ago.

"Out!"

"That's some fast limo."

His eyes darkened to stormy pools as he scowled. "Okay, okay, forget I said anything." She scurried out of the cell before he changed his mind.

"Our secretary who does dispatch doesn't come in till noon on Sunday, and the other courthouse offices here are closed. I have to get a cat out of a tree before a sixty-five-year-old woman with a heart condition goes into rescue mode. Since Jake played home-shopping network with you all night instead of catching some sleep, I hate to wake him. It's your fault so I'm drafting you to fill in."

"If there wasn't a cat and old lady involved, I might refuse."

"Then I might not let you out of jail." He gave

her a dry look. "This should take about twenty minutes. By the way, I ran the plates on the van. Not reported stolen. Contacted Delia, she doesn't remember catering a wedding. Nothing in the papers, nothing reported to the police. You sure you were getting married?"

She shrugged "Scandals in our family don't happen, and according to Norman Rockwell, cats in trees are covered by the fire department."

"It's my turn." He studied her for a moment. "The rich and powerful lead a whole different lifestyle."

"If you call being ranked below politics on my father's scale of important things a lifestyle."

"I wasn't expecting you to say that."

She shrugged. "Sometimes these things just slip out. Everyone has their limits and I've reached mine."

"Right now can you just answer the phones and stay out of trouble?"

A lock of hair fell over his forehead, giving him an innocent, boyish appearance. Hope doubted if there was anything innocent or boyish about Sheriff Clay Mitchell. He was too big, too rugged, too forceful. Forceful she'd lived with. Big and rugged were fresh territory. She looked at him out of the corner of her eyes. Nice territory. Now if she could just tape his mouth shut.

"Are you listening, Red?"

"Hanging on every word." She followed the sheriff out into the main office. What Sheriff Clay Mitchell did to a simple tan uniform was positively sinful. Her gaze traveled from broad shoulders, over muscular back to narrow waist to the nice package below. Her mouth went dry. The man looked as good going as coming.

What was she doing? Forget coming and going. Bossy men—in any way shape or male form—didn't float her boat one bit and Clay Mitchell fit that description in spades. *Remember!*

"Just take messages. Don't go anywhere."

"Aren't you worried I'll try and escape?"

"The gossips would know where you were, how you got there and what you had for lunch. Stay put."

"Gossips can do all that?"

"You've never lived in a small town, have you? If anyone needs me I'll be with Mrs. Rowley. Since her heart's been acting up, she's been living with her daughter and son-in-law and two hell-on-wheels grandkids. Everybody knows the phone number and I'll write it down for you."

"This really is your town, isn't it?"

He stopped and gazed at her. "Yeah, it is."

Hope glanced at Clay's neat organized desk. The only sound was a fax machine and an old schoolhouse clock on the far wall.

"If I hadn't kept Jake awake you would have called him?"

"Absolutely. But he comes back on duty at three.

Everybody else is at church or spending time with family. It's Sunday, so you've got phone detail.''

As he wrote the number, she looked at the open file cabinet and papers sitting on top. "Rescuing cats must be big excitement in Paradise Creek for you to be leaving in such a rush."

"When you're the sheriff, this is the way you want it to be."

"Boring?"

He arched his brow. "Safe."

The faxes being spit out were not very *NYPD Blue,* either. Halloween parades, storms over the Atlantic, and a missing-person named Jane Smith, with a fifty thousand dollar reward and Hope's picture underneath.

Holy cow! Boring vanished into thin air. Her father might have warded off a scandal, but he wasn't wasting any time tracking her down. If Sheriff Clay Mitchell spied that fax, she'd be back in D.C. before brunch. Now what? Her experience with crime was nonexistent…except in books. *Nancy Drew.* Okay, how would Nancy get out of this?

The phone rang, and when Clay picked up at Jake's desk, she did a two-finger, behind-the-back snatch of the incriminating paper. She held the picture behind her back and slow shuffled to the garbage can. Empty! Too conspicuous.

She shuffled to the file cabinet, stood in front and dropped the paper behind her back into the open drawer. As Clay talked and took notes, she eased the drawer shut with her left hip until it clicked closed.

Ta-da! Saved! She'd retrieve the paper as soon as Clay left her alone. Home free. Darn, if she wasn't the smooth one. Nancy Drew, eat your heart out.

Clay hung up and said, "There's a storm building off the coast, but it's heading out to sea. We'll probably get some rain but that's it. If anyone calls sounding nervous about the storm, tell them the weather service says everything's fine and to just carry a raincoat for the next few days."

He looked outside at the horizon. "Looks clear enough to the west and north. That's where our worst weather comes from." He seemed to be talking to himself more than her. His brows knitted together and he cracked his knuckles. A fellow knuckle-cracker, who would have thought? The one and only thing she and Sheriff Clay Mitchell had in common.

"I have a degree in social work. I can handle this."

He turned and looked her dead in the eyes. "I'm sure you have the social part down pat, but I have serious doubts about the work part."

And to think she'd admired his buns. He had flabby buns, so there. Well, not really. In fact, he had great buns. Too bad that's where his brain was most of the time.

Hope watched him leave, counted to ten to make sure he was really gone, then yanked at the drawer where she'd dropped the fax. She yanked again. Locked?

No, this was not happening. This was a small town. On TV nothing was locked up in small towns. Not houses, not cars, definitely not file cabinets.

She found a paperclip and straightened it for a jimmy just as the door opened, banging against the wall. A boy about ten years old, with hair even redder than hers, ran into the room sputtering, "Where's Sheriff Clay?"

"He's not—"

"Bobby's stuck in the roof of the old Willow Pond Church. Foot's jammed tighter than a lid on a pickle jar, and if Mom and Dad find out we were playing at that church instead of heading off to Sunday school like we were supposed to…" He swallowed and frantically looked around, "Where's Sheriff Clay?"

Sheriff Clay Mitchell, rescuer of cats and confidant of small boys. Her heart heaved an appreciative sigh. Then she remembered the *all social* and *no work* speech by the same man. Humph! She could work. In fact, she had to go to work right now or her scheme of staying incognito was history. Weren't small towns tranquil and serene? Mayberry? Fishing pole over the shoulder? Where nothing happened? She understood Clay's appreciation for boring.

She couldn't pick the lock with the boy here, and he wasn't about to leave unless his brother was safe.

Calling Clay was out—he was the last person she wanted to see.

"How long do cat rescues take?"

"Depends on the cat."

Maybe it was a mean cat. She had nothing to lose by going for Bobby. If Clay caught up with her she was dead, if she didn't get the picture she was dead. Her only hope was to get Bobby and then the picture.

"Sheriff Clay left me in charge."

The boy's eyes shot open wide. "You?"

"Yes, me," she huffed. "I'm a very capable woman."

He didn't look convinced.

"What's your name?"

"Tommy."

"How far is this church?"

"Five minutes if you take the shortcut over John's hill. Just across the street."

"You answer the phones. If anyone needs the sheriff, he's on cat recovery at Mrs. Rowley's. I'll help Bobby." *Then I'll get that darn fax out of the drawer and burn it.*

CLAY BALANCED HIMSELF on two branches of a crimson-leafed maple tree and glanced down at the woman wrapped in a black shawl who'd been his first friend in Paradise Creek, maybe his first real friend ever. "I'll have Goldie for you in a minute, Mrs. Rowley."

"Don't you go scaring my sweet precious, now. I know he can be a mite frisky."

Frisky! Goldie was a candidate for Prozac.

"Howdy, boy," came a familiar voice.

"'Mornin', Uncle Albert."

"Glad to see you earning your keep, helping out the citizens like you should. Too bad that jail of yours has gone on the fritz."

Clay edged out onto the branch. Goldie arched her back and bristled. Goldie on a power trip. "You know as well as I do there's nothing wrong with the jail, Uncle Albert."

"Must be since Mabel Farley saw that redheaded bride you locked up heading out to John's Hill. Said she's a real looker but a might too puny for jail. Couldn't you think of anything else to do with her than put her behind bars?"

"Yeah, I'm buying her a one-way ticket back to D.C. on the next bus through Paradise Creek."

What the hell was Red up to now? Where was she running off to? Did she ever do anything she was told? Clay snatched the cat and dropped to the ground. "You take care now," he said to Mrs. Rowley while handing off Goldie.

As Clay steered his cruiser toward John's Hill, a bank of clouds cut the morning sunlight by half and rain scented the air. Willow Pond Church came into view and Clay spotted Bobby, running across the field.

Clay got out of the cruiser as Bobby pulled up. "You gotta help her, Sheriff Clay. The lady with red hair like mine got me out of a hole in the roof of the church but she can't get herself down. She's behind the steeple and it's going to squall any minute."

Clay rested his hands on Bobby's shoulders. "I'll get the lady. We'll talk about you playing up here when you shouldn't later. Go home before you get soaked."

Bobby gave Clay a little smile and he stood on one foot, then the other. "She's real nice, Sheriff Clay. And she's pretty. You should ask her out on a date. Someplace fancy, with dancing. Girls like that stuff, you know."

"Go home." Clay started for the church as Bobby called, "Mama says you don't got a love-life. Dad says that's why you're crabby as a tromped-on snake, because you aren't getting any—"

"Go." He turned to see if Bobby was leaving and Bobby flashed him a man-to-man kind of grin. He was getting romance advice from a ten-year-old. Was nothing sacred in this town? Dumb question.

Thunder rumbled as Clay ran around the side of the abandoned church. He hopped weeds and brush, then spotted a ladder with more rungs gone than good. It was propped against the building and a pair of white satin high-heels were at the base. He took a few steps back and looked up. Red was perched on the apex, looking a little scared and a lot disoriented.

"What the hell are you doing up there?" Clay yelled.

"Enjoying the view. You're not invited. Go away."

She didn't look as if she was enjoying anything. Her hair floated on the gusting breeze like red silk ribbons and her arms hugged her knees. She was barefoot with one cute foot crossed over the other. Her toenails were painted bright pink. Was that a toe ring? Red didn't seem like the toe-ring or bright-pink type. Then again, she didn't seem like the kid-rescuing type, either.

"Thought I told you to stay put."

She wrinkled her nose and glared. "Neither you nor any other bigheaded man is telling me what to do. If I get killed it's my business." She heaved a sigh. "Though I would appreciate getting buried in something besides this." She yanked at the flannel shirt. "A suit from the fall Spiegel catalogue would be nice. I'd appreciate something in chocolate or rust, if you don't mind. A scarf would be an appropriate touch for the occasion."

If he'd had on a blood-pressure cuff it would have exploded. "I'm coming up."

"This roof won't hold both of us. Besides, I'm coming down...." She nibbled her bottom lip. "I really am." Her eyes darted side to side. "Soon. Very, very soon."

He went for the ladder. He had to try something.

What if she fell? He didn't want to consider that. This woman was his responsibility and she touched something in him, something besides his hormones. She was brave.

By the time he made his way to the top Red was on all fours inching backwards down the roof. Her arms trembled. "Focus on the steeple, it'll keep you oriented in a straight line. Keep coming, you're doing fine."

Much too fine. He swallowed and tried to concentrate on the bravery, but damn if she didn't have a terrific shape, and it was backing right toward him. "Go right and you'll be heading for me."

"I thought I saw bugs over there. And some green slimy stuff. I'll slip."

"I'll catch you." The well-worn denim jeans pulled tight over her backside and a jolt of pure male desire shot through him. He leaned to the side. Nice thighs, very sexy hips. She was almost to him now. "A little more right." He leaned a bit left. Just one more look at her fine backsid— The ladder swayed. *"Oh hell."*

"Whatdoyoumean, oh hell?"

She glanced back as he grabbed for the roof, snaring a fistful of rotten shingles instead. Red slid to her stomach and snatched the top of the ladder, stopping it midslide. Her eyes were wide, her breath rapid, her cheeks pink and there was a mud smear across her lower lip. She had wonderful lips, smear and all.

"*What* are you doing?"

Losing my mind over you.

"You were supposed to catch *me*. Remember?"

"Yeah." He pulled in a deep breath and steadied the ladder. This was not the time or place, but he slowly threaded his fingers through her curls. His heart sighed at the silkiness, the texture, the million shades of red and auburn flowing together as the strands slid across his palm. Her lips parted, her eyes turned smoky, like fog over the Bay at dawn. Then he kissed her, not because she'd saved his bacon, but because she was gorgeous, sassy, brave and the most exciting, fascinating female he'd ever met.

HOPE GASPED. She hadn't expected Clay to kiss her. She'd expected ranting about not calling and a whole lot of crabbiness. Not the delicious heat that warmed her all over as his kiss deepened to a mind-numbing caress. His mouth enticed, tempted, then insisted. His tongue touched hers and a quiver slid down her spine.

He tasted hot, a little dangerous, very male. She wanted more. She wanted Clay to touch her face, her neck, her breasts. For him to touch her everywhere and then…and then he'd run her life like Kenneth and her father did. They were three of a kind. That made for a winning hand in poker, but when it came to her doing what she wanted with her life, it sucked. She pulled her lips away, amazed how much she regretted doing it.

His breath was ragged, his eyes dark as midnight. "I shouldn't have done that."

But a warm spot deep down inside was thrilled to pieces he had. "You got carried away with the moment."

He arched his left eyebrow. She noticed a scar at his temple. Maybe Paradise Creek was a rougher place than she thought.

"I was the *only one* who got carried away?"

She did a mental eye roll.

"I suppose I just imagined the part about you being a participant?"

She shrugged. "'Fraid so." It was okay to lie. She would never kiss him again there was no reason to acknowledge something between them when there was never going to be a *them.* "You're not my type. You're bossy and—"

"Arrogant. I remember. And not a gentleman."

She looked into his beautiful eyes. "You came up here to get me, Clay Mitchell. That makes you a gentleman and a half."

"No, it just makes me the sheriff around here. Let's go. We're getting soaked."

"Soaked?"

"It's raining. Guess you were too *not carried away* to notice."

She followed him down the ladder, getting more soaked by the second. "I noticed. Just didn't want to make an issue of it, that's all. And I'm sitting in the front seat of your sheriffmobile whether you like it or not.''

Thunder boomed as Hope snatched her shoes and ran behind Clay, following him to the cruiser. She yanked open the passenger door and dove inside. She wiped her face and raked her hair back. ''In D.C., October is the dry season. Why are you getting so much rain over here?''

Clay wiped his shirtsleeve across his eyes. ''Good question.''

Clay started the cruiser and headed across the field, back toward town. ''Looks more like night than day.''

Lightning zigzagged across the water, thunder shook the earth. ''Makes an eerie picture.''

Picture! Her picture. The one she had to get out of that drawer. Yikes.

''Why didn't you call me to get Bobby?''

Because of that blasted fax. ''It didn't seem like a good idea at the time. Look, you take Tommy home from your office. I left him there to answer phones. Get a hot shower and dry clothes and I'll watch the phones now.''

''That's what you were supposed to be doing before.'' He pulled up in front of the courthouse.

She turned to face him. ''I won't budge this time. Cross my heart.''

''You really expect me to believe you'd rather stay right here than go to my house or Jake's and get a hot shower and into something dry yourself? You're freezing. Your teeth are chattering."

Her insides wept. She wanted a hot shower more than she wanted anything on earth...*except* for Kenneth and her father not to find her. "Bring me some clothes." She gave him her sweet-as-candy smile. "I'm just trying to help you out."

Clay's blue eyes narrowed and he put his arm across the back of the seat. She watched the windows fog so they couldn't see out. Rain fell in sheets, cutting them off from the world. "Perfect necking conditions."

She blushed from nose to toes. "I don't know what made me say that." *Like heck, it was that kiss on the roof, the one that didn't carry her away. Ha!* "Forget I said that."

His eyes darkened a shade. *Oh boy.*

He nodded toward the courthouse. "Something's going on in there, Red. What are you up to?"

"Ah, nothing." She flashed a Little Miss Innocent look to convince him. It was a look from her old life, when she really wasn't up to anything. Times sure had changed. Her innocent look cracked and she picked up her satin shoes, opened the cruiser door and tore into the building.

She sent Tommy on his way, got the blanket off the cot in the jail and wrapped it around her shoulders for warmth. Then she tackled the blasted file cabinet with her trusty paper clip. When that didn't work she tried scissors, then fist-pounding, followed by white satin high-heel shoe whacking.

"A hairpin is what you're needing, honey." Hope snapped her head up and her gaze connected with an older lady's. She wore a black hand-knit shawl with a little silver cat pin on the shoulder. She had the kindest gray eyes, eyes that reminded Hope of her own Aunt Hilda—the one person in Hope's life who hadn't been in politics.

The lady took a hairpin from her less than neat salt-and-pepper bun. "Move aside and give me some working room now."

"Why are you helping me?" Hope asked as she scooted over. "I mean, this is breaking into a sheriff's desk. We could both wind up in the jail. You don't even know me."

"I'm Lettie Rowley." The woman sat in Clay's chair and worked the lock. "You didn't know my grandson when you helped him off that rooftop. I'm just returning the favor. Besides, anything Clay has in this here drawer isn't anything the whole town doesn't know about already. Don't get me wrong, Clay's a mighty fine sheriff, but he runs things a bit too much by the book. And he sure could use a little help with his love life. It's been on the rocks since his divorce. His ex sure did a number on him. Now he claims he doesn't have time for a love life. Baloney. Everybody needs a love life, even him." She glanced at Hope. "And you." She fiddled with the pin. "And maybe me, too."

There was a click and Mrs. Rowley smiled, lighting up her whole face. "Used to pick the lock on my sister Lilly's diary when we were kids. Guess I haven't lost my touch."

Hope took out the photo, and Mrs. Rowley said, "This is you?"

"It's been a rough morning."

The door opened and Clay walked in as Mrs. Rowley yanked the notice from Hope's hand, smiled like a cat surrounded by canary feathers, then stuffed the picture under her shawl. Clay tramped across the room, touched his dripping hat in greeting to Mrs. Rowley and dropped a pile of clothes onto his desk. He turned to Hope and said, "From the school rummage sale. Best I could do."

"You must take the fastest showers in— Good heavens, is that a pair of original paisley bell-bottoms in that pile of clothes? And suede Hush Puppies and the cutest denim jacket, already frayed?"

"Red?"

Hope yanked her attention back to Clay. His look deteriorated to uncompromising sheriff and he said, "Face it, it's time for you to go home. You have no place to live, no income. You're wrapped in a blanket and wearing old clothes."

She nodded at the pants, jacket and shoes. "These

are originals. Do you know what they go for in the vintage stores?''

"Take them with you. Go home before you get caught on another rooftop." He stroked his chin. "If you really are an escaped bride I can't believe somebody isn't out looking for you."

Clay was right. Not about the rooftop, she was giving up rooftops, but about the manhunt—though it was really a womanhunt. It wasn't going to end with one fax to Clay's office. There'd be other faxes and phone calls and bulletins. How could she intercept all the things that came through this office and stay away from Clay and his to-die-for eyes and body and lips? 'Course he was also irritating as French toilet paper.

She'd have to focus on the toilet paper part.

Mrs. Rowley looked from her to Clay and smiled. "You two sure make sparks fly when you're in the same room. Haven't seen sparks fly like that in a long time."

Clay looked out the window. "It's lightning. Static electricity."

"If you believe that, Clay Mitchell, you don't have the sense God gave little green apples. And there's no need for Red to go anywhere she doesn't want to. None of us should have to do that."

Clay spread his hands, palms up. "She has no place to stay."

"That's the reason I'm here. I've decided to let this young lady stay in my family's house on Bay Street.

The Gray's still for sale, and I can't convince that thick-headed daughter of mine to live there. She likes her new fancy house and thinks my antiques are just a bunch of used furniture. Can you imagine?''

''Out of the question.'' Clay shook his head. ''You don't even know Red's real name.''

Hope said, ''I've never lived on my own before.''

''See,'' said Clay. ''She probably has maids and chauffeurs and cleaning ladies. She doesn't know one thing about old plumbing or iron skillets or how to use the generator when the electricity goes out. She'd be lost in that house, or any house where she had to fend for herself, and she needs to go back to her own home.''

Hope smiled at Mrs. Rowley. ''What if you move in with me? It's your family home. You know how to do those things. All you have to do is tell me. I love antiques. Volunteered with the D.C. Historical Society.''

Clay said, ''You don't know anything about making a home and Mrs. Rowley needs care, someone to be there for her. That's why she moved in with her daughter in the first place.''

Mrs. Rowley beamed at Hope. ''And you could help me pick out a new wardrobe, just like you did with Jake.''

Clay looked from one to the other. ''Are either of you listening to me?''

Mrs. Rowley continued to Red, ''Word's gotten

out. Everybody in town's going to be after you. I'm feeling kind of dumpy these days and I've been thinking I need a little rejuvenation. Kind of got my eye on someone.''

Clay groused, ''You're fine the way you are and you don't know Red or anything about her to be trusting her with your things and with your life. And what do you mean you've got your eye on someone?''

The older woman's brow rose and her lips thinned. She faced Clay. ''I mean I have my eye on someone. I may be a…''

''A senior,'' Hope chimed in.

''A senior,'' Mrs. Rowley echoed. ''But I'm far from dead.'' She wagged her finger at the sheriff twice her size. ''And you should remember that twenty years ago I didn't know you, either. Me and this whole town had no problem taking you in. When you showed up here you were a skinny kid, a genuine pain in the patooty, running from the law and your mama who had more time for rich men than her own son. You stole one of my Dutch apple pies right off my windowsill, as I recall. Hungry as a church mouse. Your Uncle Albert took you in and none of us knew you except that you were Albert's nephew, and he hadn't even laid eyes on you since you were a tyke.'' She nodded at Hope. ''This here woman saved my grandson. That makes her a blooming hero in my book and everyone else's in this town, and we're not likely to forget it no matter what her name is. If she doesn't want to tell it, we don't need to know. She rescued Bobby. Now put that in your pipe and smoke it.''

Hope stared at Clay, dazed. "You...You weren't born here with I Am The Sheriff Of Paradise Creek tattooed on your backside?"

Clay Mitchell had turned his life around. She admired that. He did the very thing she wanted to do. He might be the dictator of Paradise Creek, but she understood why he loved the town. It had given him a second chance. No wonder he called it *his* town.

Clay looked from Mrs. Rowley to Red. They'd bonded, like Super Glue. He wasn't going to win this fight. If he argued all day, they'd just talk around him or over him or through him. "All right, all right, Mrs. Rowley has a point."

Mrs. Rowley arched her brow. "*A* point?"

"Several points." He strode across the floor and tossed another log into the potbelly stove. He watched it catch, taking the chill out of the room. "Red's not going to run off with the Rowley family antiques."

It was the only argument he could come up with at the moment to get rid her. He couldn't very well tell the world he wanted Red out of Paradise Creek because every time he looked at her he wanted to kiss her. He needed to get rid of her before this wanting got worse.

"Even if she does have a place to live, what's she gong to do for money? Answer me that?"

"I can get a job."

"Yes, indeed," said Mrs. Rowley, looking bright and cheerful. "She can get a job right in town."

"Not much money in fashion consulting around here."

Red tipped her chin and lowered her eyes just a fraction, the way the Queen Mother probably did. "I can do other things besides consult on fashion. I've done loads of volunteer work in several fields."

Clay walked around the office, thinking about the job idea. "Volunteer work is like public service in a lot of ways," he said to himself as much as to Red. He had an idea, one with great promise. He stopped walking and smiled at her. "If you stay, you can do something to pay for the sign and fence you knocked down."

Red squinted her eyes in a suspecting manner. "How much is a sign and fence worth?"

He had her. She was as good as gone. "The price of painting the jail cells."

He watched Red closely, waiting for her beautiful face to scowl, her delectable lips to frown, her cute chin to jut in defiance. Maybe she'd even stomp her foot, the one with the toe ring. He really liked the toe ring. Sexy, very sexy. Not that it mattered because she'd be walking out of Paradise Creek and out of his life in no time. Red hated the jail. She wouldn't go there for any reason, especially to paint.

"I can do that."

He felt as if he'd been blindsided with a two-by-four. Red smiled, looking almost…relieved? "It's a great idea. Terrific, in fact. You solved my problem."

"And which of your many problems are we referring to?"

"You can pay me for watching the office when you're not here. Like I did today. You already owe me. I can fix the van before I return it to Delia."

What the hell had he missed? This had gone all wrong. "I have a secretary to answer phones. And have you ever painted anything besides your toenails? You'll have to stand on a ladder, for crying out loud. You hate heights *and* that jail. And I'm not paying you."

She pulled a pair of jeans from the pile of clothes he'd put on the desk and studied them. "It's probably against the law to not pay a worker. A sheriff shouldn't break the law. Maybe I can paint *your* office." She glanced around. "Heaven knows it needs it. Cream with navy trim and a splash of red to replicate the nautical atmosphere of the Chesapeake. You can pay me for that painting, too."

"This is not Boats-R-Us. This is the sheriff's office." How'd he get from her leaving to her staying and him paying her for the privilege?

If Red didn't leave she'd be in his office and with

him for hours and hours at a time. He'd be in a permanent state of hormonal upheaval and terminal frustration. Things had just gone from fairly desperate to plain terrible. "You have no idea how to paint."

He rummaged around in his desk for aspirin as she picked a blouse and held it up to her front. "I've watched Martha Stewart on TV—open a can, stick in a brush, put paint on the wall. It's a snap."

"Go home." *Where were the aspirin?*

She snatched the rest of the clothes from the desk and hooked her arm through Mrs. Rowley's. "I am going home, to a wonderful old house on Bay Street."

She gave a little salute as he dumped four tablets in his palm. "See you later, Sheriff Clay Mitchell. And don't forget to stop by the hardware store for paint, brushes and drop cloths."

Clay watched the door close. He swilled down the pills, then cracked his knuckles. Unless he hog-tied Red, drove her back to D.C. and dumped her by the Lincoln Memorial, she was not going home until she was good and ready. He got that message…finally. But what was *he* going to do while she was here?

If he stayed in his office while Red painted he'd go crazy, knowing how badly he wanted her. He had to get the heck out of his office. Teach safety courses at the schools, offer self-defense classes for those visiting D.C., deal with Willow Pond Church. 'Course he'd have to give Jake more responsibility since he'd cover the office. He'd have to hire another deputy to help out.

Clay swore and kicked a trash can across the office. Paradise Creek was his town, *his* responsibility and he should be the one in the office. It was either give up part of his job—the job he loved—or test his will-power to stay away from Red. Trouble was, the more he was around her the less willpower he had to test.

Starting tomorrow Jake could take over the office duties and Clay would make arrangements to have Willow Pond Church torn down. That would keep him busy and away from Red and stop anyone from ever getting trapped on that church again. It was a plan…not a perfect one, but it served the purpose. He and Red would never see each other.

Right now Paradise Creek was a novelty to her, cute little town, nice people. But she'd tire of it. She'd tire of him. Where in the heck did that come from? Red never *had* him. But if she did have him it would never last. She'd be bored out of her mind in no time with the sheriff of a small town. Elizabeth sure was. Took her less than six months to realize that high school bands were not the symphony, clam bakes were not five-star restaurants, and marrying him was the biggest mistake she ever made.

Getting together with Red would be Elizabeth all over again. And he knew that Red could never be happy in Paradise Creek.

Chapter Three

The next morning Clay watched Sam of Sam's Excavations drive his backhoe off a flatbed truck, then growl across the soggy field toward Willow Pond Church. Uncle Albert adjusted his red faded fishing hat to the back of his head, then zipped his vest against the autumn breeze. He frowned as he took a camera from his pocket. "Don't mind telling you, boy, I'm not one hundred percent sure that tearing down this church is a good idea. It's been around longer than you and me put together. A lot of people put a lot of stock in this church. Part of our roots, our beginnings."

Clay glanced at the dark line of clouds on the horizon. The smell of diesel fuel drifted his way, and he turned his attention back to the backhoe. "Tearing down the church isn't my idea of a fun day, either, but it has to be done before another kid gets a foot stuck, or worse."

Uncle Albert aimed his camera at the church and

snapped. "Losing this church is a damn shame, if you ask me. Look at those oak beams. Look at the arched doors. All hand carved."

"Look at the holes in the roof and the rotting window frames and broken glass. You know as well as I do the shame will be if someone gets hurt."

Clay pictured Red on the rooftop, saving him when he was supposed to be saving her. Snatching the ladder was quick thinking on her part, caused by lusty thinking on his part. That wasn't like him at all. He's the one who did the saving around here...until now. Mrs. Rowley was right, Red was a hero. He admired her for that, but he was pleased as a dog wagging two tails she wouldn't be around today to muddle his brain and stir up his hormones.

A siren snapped him away from his thoughts. Uncle Albert said, "Isn't that Jake's cruiser heading this way? I'd say something's up. He's driving like a maniac."

Maniac? "Ah, hell."

The cruiser screeched to a stop not far from the church and Uncle Albert. "Well if that don't beat all. Isn't that Red driving? And Lettie Rowley riding shotgun?"

"Bonnie and Clyde do Paradise Creek," Clay muttered to himself. He kicked a rock across the field, then headed for the cruiser.

As Red got out he called, "I bought your paint and brushes and rollers. You're supposed to be painting."

He saw the stubborn tilt of her chin and the fight in her eyes. Not only was she here, she was ticked off about something.

She slammed the door. "What in the world do you think you're doing out here?"

"You've moved up to stealing cruisers now?"

"Borrowing. Just borrowing, and don't try and change the subject." She planted her hands on her hips. "Mrs. Rowley pays taxes, that makes her part owner of this cruiser. She told me what you're up to. You called an emergency town council meeting this morning and railroaded through this demolition idea. Jake said I could use the cruiser since Mrs. Rowley's having second thoughts, and we needed to get here fast. He would have come himself, but he's in the middle of signing up for online law-enforcement classes."

It was shaping up to be another fun day in paradise. "What law-enforcement classes? Since when did Jake take it into his head to do something like that?"

"Since today. You're not tearing down this church."

"We need a new elementary school. We don't have money to fix the church, too. You were trapped on that roof, you know how dangerous it is. It's coming down." He took off his hat and raked his hand through his hair. "Were you this…forceful back in D.C.?"

Red had on jeans and an old green sweater that

looked soft and warm. A gold clip gathered her hair at the nape of her neck. He'd give a month's salary to undo that clip and watch those curls tumble around her face.

"Not even close. But I'm changing, and saving this church is a good reason to get…forceful. It's a landmark." She backed toward the church. "Where I come from, we don't tear them down. If you had your way, D.C. would be a pile of rubble."

She walked to the other side of the backhoe, and he lost sight of her. The backhoe suddenly stopped its forward progress.

Criminy. Now what did she do? When Clay came around, Red was sitting on the front steps of the church, between it and the backhoe. "This is no game, Red. Pick something else to change and get out of the way. The kids keep coming here when they ditch school."

"Truancy is not this church's fault. I've worked— hear that, *worked*—on a lot of restoration committees. Willow Pond Church shouldn't be razed. We'll board it up till we get the money to fix it."

"*We?* There is no *we.* This isn't your fight. You just landed here."

"I'm staying…for a while."

"Until you get bored."

"Until I get my life straightened out. I'm making this my fight. And Mrs. Rowley feels strongly about this church so I'm helping her out. It's the least I can do for someone who's been as kind to me as she has.''

"What's going on?" Uncle Albert said as he rounded the hoe with Mrs. Rowley close behind. He looked from the church to the backhoe to Red. "Well, I'll be darned. This is a sit-down, isn't it?"

"Sit-*in*," said Mrs. Rowley as she took a seat beside Red. Mrs. Rowley smoothed out her gray wool skirt and straightened her shawl.

She looked different today. What happened to her gravel-grippers? She had on shoes, real ones. Her hair was shorter, styled, no bun. Was she wearing lipstick? What had Red done to Mrs. Rowley? What had Mrs. Rowley done to Mrs. Rowley? He felt his pockets for aspirin. "No one is sitting anywhere. The church is coming down and that's final."

Uncle Albert walked up beside Red, but instead of coaxing her from the steps he sat down and linked his arm with hers. "Knocking down this church isn't right. Our great-grandpappies built it. It should stay, can feel it in my bones."

"That's arthritis. It's going to rain."

Uncle Albert turned to Red. "Isn't there some kind of protest song we're supposed to be singing? Maybe one of those Bob Dylan songs, or Peter, Paul and Mark."

Clay ground his teeth. "It's Mary," he said, totally exasperated with this whole mess. "Peter, Paul and Mary."

Uncle Albert nodded. "I think we're supposed to have flowers in our hair. Hard to find any decent flowers this time of year. Maybe we should use leaves. Too bad we don't have some beads. I kind of like beads."

Clay closed his eyes. A migraine hammered. He clenched and unclenched his fists, then refocused. "In case you've forgotten, we *all* voted on this—" he checked his watch "—less than two hours ago."

"Guess we're changing our votes, Clay. It's our right."

"What if someone gets hurt again?"

"We'll all keep an eye on the place. Got to pull together to get the job done. That's what Paradise Creek does best."

The whole damn town was crackers. Three days ago life had been so much simpler. Then Red showed up and decided to change her life, which seemed to be translating into changing the whole blessed town. *Simple* sounded really good right now.

The breeze teased Red's hair, making it swirl and shine like tiny sunbeams. His heart slammed against his ribs like a semi hitting a brick wall. She had incredible hair. Unforgettable. "I should just arrest all three of you right now, and toss your sorry butts in jail." Except Red's butt wasn't sorry at all. He'd nearly fallen off a roof observing that very fact.

Uncle Albert huffed. "You sure as hell can't go arresting your uncle and Lettie and a town hero. Why that'd look plumb terrible come election time now, wouldn't it?''

Sam killed the backhoe engine and dismounted. Uncle Albert handed him the camera. "Could you take a picture of me and Lettie and Red here? Never been in a protest before. Don't think Paradise Creek ever had a protest till now. We'll hang the picture in the town museum."

Clay mumbled, "I don't believe this," as Sam said, "Say *cheese.*"

Sam smoothed back his thinning gray hair as he returned the camera and Red said, "Willow Pond Church would qualify for the National Register of Historic Places. We can possibly get matching funds from the state if we get donations. Any chance we can turn the scheduled Halloween parade into a fund-raiser?"

Uncle Albert said, "Well, we can't go charging kiddies for walking in a parade but we can expand things a bit, like bobbing for apples, fortune-teller, haunted house, shooting range. Wouldn't take much to organize. We got time to drum up some business with the other towns between now and then. Good idea there, Red." He smiled at her, then glared at Clay. "Sure is better than leveling the place."

"I can auction off one of my quilts," chimed in Mrs. Rowley. "Red can rent herself out as one of those personal shoppers. No one in Paradise Creek has her fashion sense—I can vouch for that. Sure gives a woman a boost of self-confidence to look her best.'' Mrs. Rowley fluffed her new hairdo.

Sam said, ''I can donate one of my hunting rifles. Spot had pups, everyone wants a Chesapeake Bay retriever sired by Spot.''

Red added, ''And Clay can donate the chance to be Sheriff for a day, cruiser and all.''

''Like hell!''

''Then it's settled,'' said Uncle Albert. ''The four of us make up a majority of the town council, and Red can vote for Carlie Lewis since they look alike.''

''What in the Sam Hill does looking alike have to do with—''

''All in favor raise your hands,'' Uncle Albert said. ''All opposed? Clay, you're outvoted. Even if you do raise both hands you still only get one vote.

''Glad to be a part of this,'' said Uncle Albert as he started to walk away. ''Can I take you home, Lettie? We'll stop for coffee and some of Katie's strawberry filled doughnuts. Protesting gives me an appetite.''

He winked. ''Been too long time since we've been out together. Guess we both been taking each other for granted.'' He gave her an appreciative glance and grinned. ''Till you went and got my attention again.''

Sam said, ''I'll get some boards and tar paper and patch the hole on the roof, and I'll see what I can do about the windows.'' He started the backhoe and rumbled off.

Clay hitched his chin at the church and said to Red. "It would have been gone by now if you hadn't interfered. What did I ever do to deserve you in my town?"

"You're the one who wouldn't let me go."

Then she undid the clasp holding her hair and Clay was damn glad he'd done whatever it was to keep her here. He'd never seen a more beautiful sight than Red's curls floating on the wind. His heart stopped, he was sure of it. How could she be here tempting him when he planned so well for her not to?

"What makes you think I won't have the backhoe over here tomorrow and tear this church down?"

She looked from the church back to him. "Because the law's your life, Sheriff Clay Mitchell. Everybody knows it. Right now you're supposed to protect this church, and you'll do just that, whether you agree with the idea or not."

"I'm no saint, not even close." He wanted to touch her, he wanted to hold her, feel her in his arms, kiss her long and slow and forget where the hell she came from and who she was.

She gave him an easy smile that drove the air right out of lungs. "You're arrogant, bullheaded and think you're lord of the manor."

"So you keep telling me."

"But you're also trustworthy and dependable and honorable. Where I come from those are rare and cherished commodities, not taken for granted and held in high esteem.''

''What happened to bossy?''

''You got me at a weak moment. We just saved the church.''

Her eyes were warm as maple syrup on hotcakes, her cheeks pink from excitement and the chill in the air. She walked over to him and zipped his jacket against the breeze and turned up his collar. ''Thanks for taking care of the church, Clay Mitchell.''

She kissed him lightly on the cheek, then turned and walked to the cruiser before his head stopped reeling. His great plan to stay away from her had gone right down the tubes and he was more attracted to her than ever, even if he didn't agree with her.

He called after her, ''There's never going to be anything between us, Red.''

She glanced back and arched her brow. ''Who said there was?''

His brain was toast. Why would he say such a thing? To reaffirm to himself that it was true, that's why. Staying out of the office during the day would not work. No matter where he was she'd turn up just to throw a monkey wrench into his life. He'd have to go with plan two. Night duty. If he went on night duty he'd never see her. She'd be asleep when he was awake and vice-versa.

How long would it take Red to figure out what to do with her life and go back to D.C.? He prayed for divine intervention to descend upon her...quick. Would he be able to steel himself against her till she got to that point? He had to, especially when he knew that if he didn't the outcome would be Red leaving— and taking his heart with her.

HOPE STRETCHED her tired, sore muscles as she entered The Gray. The last two days of painting had done her in. Had it just been four days ago that she'd run away from her own wedding?

Goldie meowed and did a figure-eight welcome-home dance around Hope's ankles. She pet the cat. "Why can't I be agile like you? I hurt in places I didn't know I had."

Goldie meowed in sympathy as Hope turned on the kitchen lights, casting a golden glow over the patina cabinets, pine floor, press-backed oak chairs. "I thought painting would be easy. Martha makes it look fun. She wears these cute little smocks and smiles when she rolls the paint." Hope turned on the tap for a glass of water. "If Martha was here now I'd throw rocks at her. But it's either paint or risk going back to D.C. and I'm not ready for that yet."

As she drank the water she went over to the stack of old Nancy Drew books she and Mrs. Rowley discovered in the attic. She picked up *The Secret in the Old Clock*. "First edition. What a find. Nancy and I used to be great friends. Maybe because both of us were only daughters of single-parent fathers preoccupied with their own lives. Nancy had all the guts and I had art camp once a year in the Poconos.''

There was a note propped against the stack. It was from Mrs. Rowley and said food was in the fridge, cookies in the jar, and not to worry as she took her heart medication and she and Albert would be out late.

''Oh la la! Late's good, Goldie. With a little luck you might get a step-owner.'' She looked at the cat. ''Then again, cats don't have owners, they have staff.''

She opened a can of tuna and gave Goldie a scoop before storing the rest in the fridge. Helping Mrs. Rowley pick out some new fashionable clothes had done wonders. She looked better, acted younger and was dating. Who would have thought this might happen? Hope's smile grew. She and Mrs. Rowley did, that's who.

A twig snapped somewhere outside the house. A really big twig. Goldie stopped eating, bristled up like a scrub brush on steroids and arched his back. It could be a really big dog. A door creaked. Dogs didn't open doors and this was the front door, if she remembered the creak correctly. Footsteps sounded in the hallway, coming her way, and the silhouette of a man slid along the wall.

Hope shifted into D.C. self-protection mode. She snatched Goldie in one hand and the tin coffeepot from the stove in the other, backed to the side of the entrance and when the intruder came into the kitchen, she swung.

He ducked, but not soon enough, meeting the pot, headfirst. The lid few off and coffee spewed down his front. "Damnation!"

"Clay?"

He staggered. "What the hell are you trying to do to me?" He rubbed his forehead, then swiped coffee from his face.

Hope studied her weapon and frowned. "You dented Mrs. Rowley's antique coffeepot, and scared the bejeebers out of Goldie."

"Goldie's got plenty of bejeebers left. He'll be bejeebering for years." Clay sat down on one of the chairs and tested the lump forming over his right eye.

"Why aren't you wearing your hat? You're supposed to wear one, you know. I would have recognized your sheriff's hat. And I didn't hear the cruiser. Why are you sneaking around here anyway?" She put Goldie on the floor and went to the fridge for ice.

"I've got a news flash for you. Sneaks don't walk in through the front door. Besides, Paradise Creek doesn't have sneaks. Everybody already knows about everybody else so there's no need, and I left my hat in the cruiser parked over on Main."

"If I put your shirt in cold water the coffee won't stain." She dumped ice in a dishtowel and went to Clay. "Why are you here, anyway?"

"One reason is to give you this." He reached into

his shirt pocket and pulled out a star covered in aluminum foil. "From Bobby. Since you saved him from the rooftop, he thinks I should make you a deputy. He's been after me to get you a cruiser. Nothing small-time about Bobby."

Hope stared at Clay, then took the star. "What a nice thing for him to do. I'm...touched." She grinned as she ran her finger over the points. "Did you tell him I'd be deputy when pigs fly?"

Clay gently captured her chin between his thumb and forefinger and tipped her face down to his. His eyes were dark with sincerity, his chin firm and direct. "What you did was incredibly brave. No one would think otherwise, especially me. Bobby could have been hurt but you got him off that roof before he was. You're afraid of heights and you put his welfare before your own. That impresses me more than you know."

Guilt nipped at her conscience. "Ah, there was a little more to it than that. I haven't told you the whole story. You know how you said you weren't a saint, well move over."

"You're courageous."

"Desperate."

"You can be a deputy of mine anytime."

He gave her a slow smile, the touch of his fingers heating her skin. His gaze connected with hers, and her heart beat double-time. His eyes darkened a shade more and he took his star from his shirt and pinned her foiled one to her blouse with it. She licked her suddenly parched lips. His arrogance she could dismiss as being typically Clay Mitchell, someone she wanted no part of. But tenderness and gratitude were not so easily put off. It made him understanding, vulnerable. Sheriffs weren't vulnerable. She'd have to remember this one was, at least a little. And it touched her heart more than she thought possible.

"That coffee stain's going to set." Her voice sounded strange, even to her own ears.

He let go of her, but their stare held as he took off his tan uniform shirt, leaving him in a white T-shirt. "Giving you Bobby's present isn't the reason I came here since I didn't know you'd be here. I ran into Mrs. Rowley at Lickity Splits. She and Uncle Albert were sharing a hot fudge sundae. She said she might have left the light and the oven on and you were still working, and could I please come here and check on it because she and Albert were taking in a movie and they didn't want to miss the beginning."

Hope reached for the shirt. Their fingers touched and he didn't pull back. She swallowed hard. "Was…was she wearing the lilac or the periwinkle dress?"

"Lilac. I think. Do you realize there's more paint on you than on the walls of the jail?"

"The lilac brings out the soft silver in Mrs. Rowley's hair." Clay had gorgeous hair. "Why does your T-shirt have *Annabelle Lee* printed on it? Your ex?"

Why do I care?

"Uncle Albert's crabber. A boat. Named after his wife who died long before I showed up. He worked the Bay for crabs and oysters for twenty-five years. Tough work. Dangerous as hell. He gave me a home when I didn't have anyplace to go."

"That's why you stay in Paradise Creek?"

"One of them."

"Loyalty must by your middle name, Clay Mitchell."

Surprise touched his face.

"You know, I told Mrs. Rowley when I'd be home. She knew I'd be here and she never leaves the oven on."

He studied her from head to foot, though she barely noticed because his T-shirt accented every wonderful muscle from broad shoulders to firm pecs to narrow waist. It also emphasized the sort of man he was, and that included more than his physical attributes. It gave her a little glimpse of his soul.

He said, "I have a funny feeling about this."

She had a funny feeling, too. It was a deep-inside feeling. It wasn't a ha-ha feeling. It was hot and sexy and getting hotter and sexier the more she looked at Clay and he looked at her.

"I think we've been set up. I think Mrs. Rowley sent me over here to run into you, though not quite so literally."

Clay took her hand that held the ice and lifted it to his forehead where she'd whacked him.

"Why?" It should be against the law for a man to look this buff.

"She's trying to get us together like you're helping her get together with Uncle Albert."

Clay's eyes reflected the inner man, the man not many saw. The rest of his face could be unreadable, business, all sheriff, but never his eyes. Every emotion was right there—happiness, anger, determination, arrogance, desire. Right now there was definitely desire.

"You think so?" She slowly traced his lips with her index finger. First the top with the thin scar on the left side, then the bottom. Both were delectable, enticing, totally irresistible.

He nipped her finger, and her insides ignited.

"Her plan worked." He swiped paint from Hope's cheek and looked at the smear on his thumb. He took the towel from her hand, tossed it into the sink, then he encircled her waist with his arm and sat her on his lap. They were eyes-to-eyes, nose-to-nose, mouth-to-mouth. His breath mixed with hers. "Remind me to thank Mrs. Rowley."

Then he kissed her.

No one on earth kissed like Clay Mitchell. The kitchen tilted just a bit, her brain tilted a lot. She'd wanted this kiss since Clay kissed her on the church roof. His tongue teased her lips, her mouth opened in response. She wrapped her arms around him, feeling the strength in his shoulders and back. The warmth of his flesh seeped into hers.

She had the sudden urge to undress him head to toe, see every gorgeous muscle up close and personal. His hands skimmed up her sides to her breasts. His thumb brushed her left nipple and she nearly slid onto the floor.

His kiss deepened and a moan of pure ecstasy crept up her throat. She ran her fingers through his silky hair, licked the lobe of his right ear and saw Mrs. Rowley outside the kitchen window holding a tabloid with Hope's picture and the headline Senator's Daughter On The Lam.

Yikes! Was life ever fair? She didn't want to deal with being a daughter on the lam right now. She wanted to make out with Clay. But if she didn't do something about the stupid paper, Clay would see that headline and personally escort her back to her father. She broke the kiss and pulled in a deep breath. "You have to go."

"G-go? Now?"

She stood up and tugged on his arm. "Come on, come on. Hurry it up. You have to get out of here right now."

He looked as dazed as she felt. "Does this have something to do with my being bossy? Because I really didn't think—"

"Believe it or not, it has nothing to do with that."

She snapped his shirt from the floor and draped it over his left shoulder, then pulled him to a standing position. "It's…because you're on duty. What we're doing is not duty. You'll probably get fired. It could be ugly."

"I will? It will?" She tugged him down the hall to the front door. "Who are you planning to tell?"

"We shouldn't be in Mrs. Rowley's kitchen necking. It's not very sheriff-like. What if you did this with everyone? What kind of town would this be."

"I don't do this with everyone. Mrs. Rowley doesn't care that I'm here. Hell, she sent me here. She's the one who set us up. Remember?"

"Things change." Hope yanked open the front door. "You wouldn't believe how much things change." She got behind Clay and pushed him out onto the front porch. "See you later. Oh, and just put that shirt in cold water with a little shampoo. The maid swears it cleans everything."

She closed the front door with him standing on the front porch. She tore for the back door, smoothing her hair and fighting for some composure as she went. She let in Mrs. Rowley and Albert, not without a twinge of disappointment. As much as she liked them, they were a poor substitute for necking with Clay Mitchell.

Hope took the paper from Mrs. Rowley's hand and snapped it open. "I'm on the front page of a national tabloid? Isn't there anything more important going on? Isn't Oprah doing anything this week?''

Mrs. Rowley touched the stars on Hope's shirt, the one Bobby had made, then Clay's official one. "Guess this makes you an official deputy around here."

"Not exactly." More like an official dope for getting involved with Clay in the first place. There was no logical reason for her to fall for him, none at all. It was a dumb, dumb, dumb thing to do. So why was she doing it anyway?

Uncle Albert said, "We came across the paper at Lickity's. It was a stroke of luck that Clay didn't see it when he was there, but we bought up all they had in case he came back that way again. We should go to Phil's Fill 'er Up to get the rest of these. The only other place that sells this rag is Katie's Kitchen and you can get there as soon as it opens in the morning."

Hope pointed to the paper. "I appreciate all you're doing, but it's too late. Even if Clay hasn't seen this article someone else in town must have. They'll turn me in. I'm doomed."

Mrs. Rowley wagged her head and smiled hugely. "Not if you don't want to be, dear. See, Paradise Creek isn't like most other places. You saved one of our own, then figured out how to save Willow Pond Church. You've given out lots of fashion advice. We like you being here and no one cares what your name is. You've given to this town and the only thing you're asking in return is a little privacy. 'Course Clay would hand you over in a New York minute because he'd think it's his duty as sheriff and all.''

Uncle Albert said, ''Everything's going to be fine as frog's hair if we get a move on now and get what papers we can before Clay comes across them. We'll meet again at first light to get the rest.'' He patted Hope's arm. ''You'll see, everything'll work out. This is Paradise. What could go wrong?''

CLAY STOOD in the doorway of the only house he'd ever thought of as home. The dawn cast pink and purple across the sky, mist billowed over the wide expanse of open water before him. *Red sails at morning, sailors take warning.* More rain on the way. He quietly crossed the porch so as not to wake Uncle Albert, descended the steps and crossed Bay Street. Dew shimmered in the grass, collecting on his boots and pant cuffs. He made his way to the shore as he'd done thousands of times before.

Every day for twenty years he'd thanked the heavens he wound up living on this side of the Bay and not the other. He picked up a rock, checked for roundness and flatness like Uncle Albert had taught him, and skipped it across the dark blue surface, watching it disappear into the fog. For him there was no better place on earth than Paradise Creek, no better job than being sheriff and protecting the people who lived here.

A few raindrops fell, a line of gray clouds building on the horizon. He could control a lot of things in this town, but not the weather and not Red. That woman made him crazier than a waltzing pig.

In spite of both of them knowing they were not suited for one another at all, last night she'd matched him kiss for kiss, feel for feel, and then…and then she tossed him out on his ear. No spiel of why she shouldn't get involved with him. This time she gave some story that made no sense, then slammed the door in his face.

It was as if she was suddenly…*bored.* Elizabeth got bored with him and Paradise Creek in less than a year. With Red it had taken less than a week, and she wasn't just bored with him in general but last night she'd been bored with his kissing. At first things were going well, very well, than all of a sudden she seemed preoccupied and tossed him out.

And this wasn't the first time. Up on the roof of the church she said she wasn't carried away by his kiss.

What didn't she like? Wrong pucker? Wrong angle? Too gentle? Too ravishing? Damn, he was a good kisser, least he had been. What was wrong with him now? And how in the hell did he intend to fix it?

Chapter Four

A half hour later Clay headed for Katie's Kitchen. He couldn't sleep. Standing in the rain and grinding his teeth over his kissing problem was pointless, but losing himself in a pile of artery-clogging eggs and bacon might help. Maybe that was it. Maybe his kisses needed help. A tonic. Was there a kissing tonic?

Hellfire! He was thirty-two years old. He should know how to kiss at thirty-two. Should be in the prime of his damn kissing-life and not thinking about a tonic. Was he on a downward kissing spiral and destined to be the worse kisser on the Eastern Shore?

He pushed open the café door and inhaled the familiar aroma of fresh coffee and pastries that fed the soul as much as the body. The usual clatter of dishes and utensils coming from the kitchen soothed his bewildered condition.

The Jones brothers hunched over coffee and doughnuts at the counter. Ruth Owens and Willa Jenkins greeted him pleasantly enough, then exchanged haughty looks with each other. Would the rivalry over the *best pumpkin pie* ever end?

Sam, Carlie Lewis and Mabel Farley stood by the cash register with Red. She wore a sweatshirt, painter's hat and jeans showing more paint than material. A ribbon held her hair at the nape, her skin fresh and clean. She stuffed a bag full of newspapers, probably to use to protect his office against her pitiful painting skills. But there was nothing pitiful about her as a woman. The smoldering heat in his gut fired hot.

So, she thought he couldn't kiss, did she? Thought he had no sex appeal, could kick him to the curb, that he was boring. Since his decision to steer clear of Red was already shot to hell his wounded male ego demanded satisfaction.

He tossed his hat onto the nearest table, knocking over the salt and pepper shakers and sending little packets of sugar flying. He stomped over to Red, gathered her in his arms, tipped her back just a bit and kissed her for all he was worth.

HOPE GASPED IN SURPRISE, giving Clay full access to her mouth as well as her lips. What the heck was he doing? Then his tongue mated with hers and she didn't have to contemplate that question again. Shock waves radiated from her head to her toes and every inch in-between. They were big shock waves since they'd started last night when sitting on Clay's lap, and hadn't subsided one bit. His fingers cupped her head as if laying claim to her, his other hand embraced the small of her back bringing her body tight to his. Her breasts swelled against his muscular chest and his lips molded to hers.

A warm spot swirling deep inside ever since she laid eyes on Sheriff Clay Mitchell ignited into a blazing inferno. This was the best she'd ever felt in her life and she didn't want it to stop. She wanted to wrap her arms around him, be a full participating partner, show Clay how much she appreciated this kiss, especially since they were interrupted last night.

But she couldn't let go of the blasted bags she held in each hand. Spilling them all over the floor and giving Clay full view was the last thing she needed. She needed to get out of here now, before Clay's kiss made her forget she came to Katie's to get rid of tabloids that threatened to send her back to D.C.

But why was *he* here when he was supposed to be on night duty? And why was he kissing her in front of so many people?

He broke the kiss and gazed down at her. His eyes bright with passion, his breath hot and fast across her lips. "Well, damn."

His heart beat wildly against hers. Everyone in the diner stared slack-jawed and openmouthed. Sam said, "Jumpin' Jehosaphat, that's one way to start off the morning right. Yessiree. Sure beats the heck out of cereal and vitamins. Nice way to get a little exercise. Lot more interesting than jogging."

Carlie and Katie let out wolf whistles. Mabel and the Jones brothers clapped and Billy Jones said, "Sure wish I was in your place, Clay."

Clay gave Billy a hard look. "I needed to see if… I wanted to know if…" He shifted his weight from foot to foot and looked at Red. "It was personal, okay?"

Hope gripped her bags tighter so as not to drop them in her lusty state of confusion. "This will be all over town before noon."

He massaged the back of his neck. "More like before breakfast. How…how was it?"

"How was what?"

"The *kiss,* dammit, the *kiss?*"

"Good grief." It was great, terrific, wonderful! But she wasn't about to say that in a roomful of people who considered gossip a sporting event. She had to ditch these papers right now before the sheriff part of Clay Mitchell kicked in and realized something was going on at Katie's Kitchen besides bacon and eggs and making out. She stepped around Clay and made for the door.

A misty rain blanketed the street gluing leaves to the sidewalks and putting a damp chill in the air. She slid one bag of papers inside the other, gripped the bag tight against her chest so as not to lose any, then hurried past the still-dark storefronts that stood like soldiers guarding Main Street. But before she was halfway down the deserted block she heard Clay calling, "Wait up."

She glanced back and saw him heading her way. *Wait?* When she needed to run away from him not only to get rid of the papers but take the edge off her present state of sexual exasperation which he caused *again.* As he pulled up, she hunched over the bag to hide the contents and keep it dry.

"I'm sorry I upset you. I had no right to kiss you back there."

"You know that everyone in Paradise Creek will think there's something going on between us when there's not."

He gave her a hard look. "Why do you care so much what everyone thinks all of a sudden?"

She looked skyward for strength. "Because, Mr. Sheriff, now this whole town is going to try and get us together. Mrs. Rowley and Uncle Albert started already and they didn't have any ammunition like kissing in Katie's Kitchen at 6:00 a.m. No one seems to get the message that you're way too bossy for *me* and *I* remind you too much of your ex." Hope shrugged and gave him a little grin. "She must have been a delightful woman."

"Oh yeah. She was damn terrific, for about six months."

The rain went from mist to drizzle. The front of the bag went from tan to dark brown, sopping up the water. She held the bottom so the papers wouldn't break through. "I've got to go. We'll talk later."

"Here, let me take that." He snatched the bag from her hands and tucked them under his arm, making Hope's heart leap into her throat. "I'll walk you to the office."

"No need." The bag ripped down the side. Papers dangled revealing her left ear and eye. "Don't you have work to do instead of walking with me?" She reached for the bag. "Doesn't somebody need arresting? What about tickets? It'll be rush hour soon and everybody will be speeding and just think of all those—"

He stopped dead and looked down at her. Raindrops clung to his hair. He'd forgotten his hat again. His eyes were blue as any ocean and his chin had a hint of morning stubble. What would it feel like against her lips, to taste him with the tip of her tongue? Rough? Warm? A little dangerous? Sexy! Should she wrestle him to the ground and find out?

"Do you see any rushing or speeding going on here? Tell me, just for the record, does kissing me have any affect on you whatsoever, other than to make you run away from me and spout nonsense?"

If he only knew. 'Course that would create more problems than it would solve since more kissing would just lead to more frustration, and she was frustrated enough. The other side of the bag began to tear.

Clay shifted it from one arm to the other, revealing her picture from the nose up. *Yikes.*

"I have to get to work, I need the newspapers to…to cover the floor. You don't want me to get paint on your floor, do you? And I think you're a fantastic sheriff, a remarkable kisser and to be congratulated on not having a rush hour. I'll try and refrain from spouting. *Now give me the blasted bag.*"

"I think I'll become a monk." He slipped his free arm around her and kissed her till her toes curled and her senses were numb. He heaved a deep sigh and rested his forehead against hers. "I'd make a really lousy monk."

He handed her the bag and left, retreating into the swirling fog.

Hope felt light-headed, woozy, almost weak. She steadied herself against the light post for a moment, then headed for the courthouse. All she'd wanted to do this morning was get rid of the tabloids. Instead Clay had arrived on the scene and thrown everything into a tizzy. A tizzy that was a carryover from last night's tizzy.

Whoever said life in a small town was boring had never run away to Paradise Creek and been kissed by Sheriff Clay Mitchell. She couldn't think straight when he was around. Heck, she couldn't think period.

By the time she got to the sheriff's office her clothes were damp from the rain and her brain was the consistency of oatmeal. Mrs. Rowley, Uncle Albert and Jake were discussing Halloween Parade plans and Uncle Albert said, "Nothing like a good old-fashioned parade to bring the town together. Yep, parades, weddings and funerals are the best for that. Bet half the folks in town met their mates at one of those functions or the other."

Hope stepped over a drop cloth and plopped the bag of soaked papers down on Jake's desk. She took off her hat, undid her ribbon and shook her hair free. "How are we going to get rid of these things? It's a little risky to be burying them behind the jail."

"The janitor over at the elementary school is burning them in the school incinerator. His great-granddaddy was a preacher at Willow Pond Church, you see. Pleased as a clam at high tide that you saved the place. Heard you and Clay ran into each other over at Katie's."

Jake handed Hope a towel. "Clay ran into me." She nodded toward the desk. "He took that bag and I nearly had a heart attack on the spot."

Mrs. Rowley tossed Hope a saucy smile and winked at Uncle Albert. "Heard that's not all he took."

Hope stopped drying and stared at the three of them. "How'd you know about it already? And it was just a kiss, one I didn't plan on or provoke, I might add."

"And one you didn't fight off, either," added Uncle Albert on a chuckle.

"I had my hands full, with the papers."

"Some are saying you were downright receptive. We heard about that kiss, too. It's been a mighty interesting morning in Paradise Creek."

Jake said, "Clay's a great guy, a fine sheriff, keeps everything around here running smooth and safe."

Mrs. Rowley added, "And he's mighty handsome to boot. I think he's sweet on you."

"Guess that's why he locked me in jail."

Jake said, "He gave you his star, didn't he? He wouldn't do that to just anyone. Fact is, I can't ever remember him doing that before. And when you're around he's not nearly so bossy with the rest of us. Too busy thinking about you, I guess. You're good for him and that makes things good for the town."

Hope headed toward the heavy oak door that separated the office from the jail cells. She poured parchment-white paint into a pan and grabbed a roller. She stopped for a moment and felt in her front pocket for the sheriff's star Clay had given to her. She knew it wasn't something he parted with easily, probably never had before just like Albert said. But that didn't mean there was anything between her and Clay. He was just grateful over her rescuing Bobby.

She went back into the office and glared at the three people sitting there. "What you all mean is Clay and I are so busy butting heads and getting in each other's way he's not butting heads with you all and getting in your way."

"That, too," Jake said. "But it's not the only reason you two should get together. You keep each other hopping. Keep the juices flowing, if you know want I mean."

Hope jabbed the roller into the pan, then on to the wall. "The only juice I'm interested is from fruit. Clay Mitchell is not the man for me. He's the sheriff around here, he tells people what to do and it doesn't stop when he takes off that uniform. Clay is a natural-born boss but I refuse to let him boss me."

She tried to ignore the star in her pocket, pressing against her thigh. "I've had men tell me what to do my whole life and I'm not getting mixed up with another one who wants to do it all over again."

"That decision seems to have upset you a bit, dear. You just painted my purse."

Hope rolled more paint and the star seemed to press a bit harder. "There will be no more incidents to report from Katie's Kitchen or The Gray."

"Do you know you just painted over the window, dear?"

"I want to lead my own life. Clay would make my life a complete disaster."

"Dear, I think the disaster is this office. You just painted the top of Clay's desk."

She plopped the roller in the pan, splashing paint everywhere. She looked at Mrs. Rowley. "Do not try and get me and Clay together. It won't work. He is absolutely *not* the man for me."

And her opinion hadn't changed one iota by the time she left the courthouse at six. She'd give her new Gucci bag for ten minutes in a hot tub right now, but she had to settle for washing up in the back room. The only bright spot was she'd been invited to Ruth Owens's for dinner along with a promise that Clay Mitchell had not been invited, too. The citizens of Paradise Creek were a crafty lot and matchmaking was a favorite pastime. After the Katie's Kitchen episode she and Clay were prime candidates, but this dinner was safe. Least it was worth the gamble since Ruth's pumpkin pie was legendary. To hear Jake talk, Shakespeare would have written sonnets about this pie. She didn't share Bill's gift of poetry, but she'd sure eat her share of pie. She was starved.

When she got to Ruth's little yellow clapboard on Emerson, a note on the front door said, "Come on in."

She entered and followed her nose to the kitchen that beckoned—make that seduced—with smells of brown sugar and cinnamon and nutmeg and a dash of allspice. Her taste buds went on high-alert. She tried to taste the aroma. She licked her lips in anticipation.

The table was set for two. Good sign, no Clay. Not only because matchmaking was out, but because that meant half the pie was hers. Whipped cream? Did Ruth make fresh whipped cream? If Clay did show up, she's simply plead a headache and leave...and take the pie with her. "Hello? Anybody home?"

"Red?"

She should have known. Clay. She'd been duped. She could leave, but... She took another sniff.

She heard some scuffling by the sink and walked around to the other side of the table. She looked down and saw half of a man lying on the floor, his other half under the sink. Only one man on planet earth had a torso like that. "What are you doing?"

"Hand me the wrench by my leg."

"How about a screwdriver, I know what that looks like—"

"The thing that has a *C* on top."

She handed it over. Metal scraped against metal followed by some creative swearing. "There, got it."

The torso moved forward and Clay appeared, inch by wonderful inch—broad chest, strong shoulders, firm neck determined chin and oh-so-handsome face. "What were you doing in there?"

"Fixing Ruth's sink."

Hope's eyes widened. "Sheriffs do plumbing work, too?"

He stood and shrugged. "For some of Ruth's pie I'd do darn near anything." His eyes narrowed. "What are you doing here?"

"How much of the pie did she promise you?"

He looked at the sink. "Plumbing prices are high these days. Uncle Albert's out with Mrs. Rowley. All of it."

"That's my pie."

"What did *you* do to earn it?"

Hope gave him her best defiant look, hoping it carried some clout. "She invited me for dinner."

"Inviting takes second place to plumbing." He walked to the table.

"Touch that and…I'll paint your potbelly stove."

He turned and glared. "You wouldn't."

"We're talking pumpkin pie here." She looked around. "Where *is* Ruth?"

"I'm no Sherlock Holmes but my guess is this was a setup—since there was nothing wrong with the sink—and Ruth's gone. Getting us together would put her on the top rung of the gossip ladder."

Hope went to the stove. "Pot roast. Medium-well. New potatoes, fresh peas, mushrooms. Big ones. Mrs. Rowley's out with Uncle Albert. If I go home it's an egg sandwich. There're warm rolls and homemade apple butter."

Clay leaned against he sink and folded his arms. "I'm not leaving. I've been smelling this dinner for an hour now. Setup or not, a man can only stand so much."

"If we stay, the matchmakers win."

"Hell of a price for pot roast and pumpkin pie."

"Speak for yourself, Clay Mitchell." Hope grabbed a plate from the table and headed for the stove. She dished up the meat and veggies and gravy and two rolls and a dollop of apple butter and sat down.

Clay sat across from her, his plate piled as high as hers. She dug in. It was orgasmic. Her eyes flew open and she stared at Clay. She swallowed a mushroom whole.

Clay looked up from his scarfing. "What? You don't like it?"

"It's…wonderful." Being this near to him, thinking orgasmic thoughts was…unnerving. Suggestive. Did Ruth put extra pepper in this roast?

Clay stabbed a carrot. "What are you staring at."

His eyes fused with hers across the table. The carrot somersaulted back to his plate. He lowered his fork.

She swallowed. "Not as hungry as I thought."

He let out a deep breath. "This won't be the last time we get set up." He sat back in his chair and fiddled with his napkin.

"What should we do?"

"Send you back to D.C."

"Hey, I didn't get us into this mess, you did with that kiss at Katie's Kitchen. You go to D.C. I'm staying here till I figure out how to tell my dad to butt out of my life and what size rope I need to string up my fiancé."

"Ex-fiancé and can't you tell your dad now?"

"I'm getting there. In the meantime we should just stay away from each other. Just because we're attracted doesn't mean we should act on that attraction. Right?"

He snarled. "What do you think I've been *trying* to do? I stayed out of the office and I took the night shift. You're not for me, I'm not for you. But sometimes…" He stood and looked out the window over the sink.

"Sometimes what?"

The only sound was the tick of the schoolhouse clock by the back door. "Sometimes my lips don't seem to get the message."

Boy, did she know that feeling.

She stood. "You're right. We need to stay apart and with both of us in on the plan now it should work."

"And you'll have time to focus on getting your life together and going back to D.C."

"Why are you in a hurry to get rid of me?"

He gave her a sideways look. "There's nothing or anyone interesting enough to keep you here. Everything is picturesque and right out of Norman Rockwell. Works for a while, then you'd be bored out of your mind."

"It works for you."

"It wouldn't work for you."

"It must be wonderful to be so right all the time." She turned and stomped to the front door, turned again and went back to the kitchen. The pie was hers, darn it.

Clay stood by the sink, still staring out the window. Something was wrong, there was something he wasn't telling her and probably not telling anyone else, either. Clay Mitchell wasn't exactly the whiney type. The pie didn't look so great after all. Neither did the pot roast. Clay did. Drat. She turned and walked away. She'd looked forward to tonight and now he'd put her in a rotten mood. Good thing they were staying apart. She didn't like this mood at all.

AS CLAY HEADED for the sheriff's office to take over night duty he'd never been in such a rotten mood. He should be in a good mood, dammit. He checked his watch. He hadn't seen Red in three days, two hours and fifteen minutes, since they didn't have dinner together at Ruth's. Staying away from Red should make him content. But he wasn't.

The fact that his desktop was now painted parchment-white and that Red had painted everything in the whole blasted office white—except his potbelly stove—added to his mood. But that wasn't the cause.

Clouds and rain made everything gloomy, reflecting his disposition. He eyed the car parked at the curb, frowned and took his citation pad from his pocket.

His stopped writing the citation and his chest tightened. This was the exact spot where he'd kissed Red after the Katie's Kitchen incident. He thought of Red in his arms—actually it was his *arm* because the other held the bag of papers. He wanted to kiss her again. He'd give a month's salary for just one of her kisses.

Uncle Albert tramped his way. "What do you think you're doing, boy?"

"Writing a ticket for your broken windshield here. Your car's not in proper running order."

Uncle Albert turned his collar against the evening air. "It's not a crack, it's a chip the size of a nickel."

"Will be a crack soon. It's dangerous. Could hamper your vision." Clay continued to write as raindrops speckled his paper.

"For crying in a bucket, it's in the corner, on the passenger side. For the last three days you've been completely loony, you know that. Can't believe you gave me a ticket this morning for crossing the street."

"Jay-walking. You should have used the crosswalk."

"It was 6:00 a.m. The only thing moving on this here street was Lettie's cat. Willa Jenkins said you gave her a ticket for speeding."

"She could have been hurt."

"She was riding her bike, up a hill. She's seventy years old."

"She needed to slow down. She could have a heart attack or stroke. I've ordered a traffic light for Main Street, that should slow things down a bit, especially during rush hour."

"R-rush hour?"

"We could have a rush hour."

"Traffic light? In Paradise Creek?" Uncle Albert ran all ten of his fingers through his graying hair, giving himself an Einstein hairdo. "That's it! I can't take any more. You and Red have sent this town into a complete dither. Neither of you have made one lick of sense since that dinner at Ruth's."

"Red and I don't want to be matched. We want to…be left alone. As in staying apart."

"Yeah, that's made both of you happy. The whole town's giddy over your wonderful moods. Do you know Red painted the drinking fountain in the hall purple?"

Uncle Albert stuffed his hands in his pockets. "Jake wants to see you before he leaves for the night. He has a problem. We all have a problem."

"What problem? The only thing I can think of is all this damn rain. Not much we can do about that except keep our fingers crossed that it stops." Clay ripped the citation from the pad and handed it to Uncle Albert.

Uncle Albert frowned and shook his head as he studied the pink paper. He pulled in a deep breath. "It's not the rain. Jake thinks he has a solution." Uncle Albert looked at the citation again. "Didn't think much of it at first but it's growing on me. More and more. Come along, boy. There's work to be done."

"I've got more work to do here. So little time, so many tickets." Clay started down the street.

"Heard tell Red's aiming to paint your potbelly stove before she leaves this evening. White. With some posies on the side. What do you think about that, huh?''

Clay stopped. He turned on his heel and stuffed his citation pad in his back pocket. ''That stove's been in the sheriff's office as long as Paradise Creek's had a sheriff, and it sure as hell's never been painted parchment-white with flowers. What is she thinking?''

''At this point it's anybody's guess.''

Clay followed Uncle Albert into the courthouse past the purple drinking fountain and into Clay's office that was more Jake's than Clay's. The place looked like a damn hospital. He greeted Mrs. Rowley and asked, ''Are you here about the problem? What's Jake's solution?''

''More my solution than Jake's.'' She beamed. ''Albert didn't think so, but it looks like he's changed his mind. I'm guessing you must have done something plain awful to get him to come around.''

Clay was too tired to try and unravel that piece of information, and he hadn't a clue what this new problem was. Had someone told him about it before? He didn't think so, but his brain wasn't working too well because all he thought about was Red.

He tried to put her out of his mind. He'd worked like a dog so he wouldn't think about her during night duty, and in hopes of being so tired he'd sleep when his shift was over. Fat chance that. The more he tried to forget about Red, the more she popped into his mind.

Clay said to Jake, ''Where's the mad painter? We can discuss this problem as soon as I talk to her.''

''She's in back, in the storage area with her cans and brushes and rollers. It's her shrine. Least the place is getting cleaned up. Sure better than it was before.''

''That's what I want, all right, a jail known for its fine decor. Why did I ever agree to her doing this?'' He ran his hand over his face. ''Hell, it was my idea. The woman's out of control.''

Mrs. Rowley fiddled with a button on her blazer and pursed her lips. ''She's not the only one.''

Clay stuffed his hands in his pockets. ''What's that supposed to mean?''

''Nothing at all, dear. Go find Red. Hurry. Please hurry. If we don't do something, this problem could get worse and then I don't know what we'll do.'' She shooed him away as if he were some pesky fly.

Clay gave Jake and Uncle Albert and Mrs. Rowley a hard look and rocked back on his heels. ''Something's going on here. You all look as guilty as sin.''

Jake nodded toward the little stove. ''She's mixing, Clay. She'll be out here with her magic roller any minute now and there'll be no stopping her once she gets started. Trust me, I know. I've been watching her for days now. It's downright scary.''

Clay walked from the office area back to the cells.

"Red? Where the hell are you? What do you think you're doing, painting my stove and—"

The oak door suddenly slammed closed behind him. Clay spun around and stared at it, not quite believing what had happened. When he looked back, Red was standing beside him. Least he assumed it was Red. With all the paint on her face it was hard to tell, though there were little sprigs of white splattered red hair sticking out from under her baseball cap and, of course, there were the green eyes. He'd recognize those anywhere.

She asked, "What are *you* doing in here?"

"Looking for you." He glanced back to the door, then tried the knob. Locked. Big surprise there. "Working late?"

"Jake said I missed some spots in the back cell and I needed to touch them up. I was looking for the spots before I cleaned up all the cans and stuff in here. Though with all the paint I've used it's hard to imagine that I missed anything."

"Amen to that!"

"Why is the door shut? Are you here on official business or what? We—as in you and me—" she poked him in the chest with her finger leaving a white round fingerprint "—are staying away from each other. That was the agreement. Remember?"

"Yeah, I remember but the three on the other side of that door and the whole blessed town don't agree."

"It's locked?"

"Bingo."

"Matchmaking?" Red scrunched up her face in question. She looked like a mime. But damn if he didn't want to kiss her anyway. He'd missed her. Missed her more in three days than he'd missed most people in a lifetime.

"Master class."

Uncle Albert called, "Clay? Red? Are you two in there?"

Clay slammed his hand against the door. "Where the hell else would we be?"

"Don't get testy. But, now that we've got your attention I guess you should know that you're staying in that there jail till you straighten things out between you. Lettie and Jake and I will be back tomorrow to see how you're doing and whether you figured out a plan for getting along. Everybody in town thinks you'd make a great couple but if that's not what you want, fine. You should know that we're not springing you till you both get into a better disposition and stop driving the rest of us loco."

Clay pounded his fist on the heavy oak door, again. "You can't lock up a sheriff in his own jail."

But all he got for an answer was the shuffle of feet on the other side and the closing of the door leading into the hallway. "Mrs. Rowley? Jake? Uncle Albert? Somebody out there better answer me or...or ah, damn it all!"

Chapter Five

Clay listened at the heavy oak door for any movement on the other side, till Red said, "What did you do to get us in here, Clay Mitchell?" She gave him a beady-eyed look. "You bossed somebody around once too often, that's it. Or was it the traffic-light idea? I knew that would cause World War III around here. You've been completely irrational lately, and I can understand why the town is mad at you. But why me?"

"*I'm* irrational?" His voice echoed and he took a step away from the door, nearly tripping over a paint can. He glared at the can, then at her. "You think us getting locked up together in jail happened because of me? Because of how *I'm* acting? Now there's a good laugh. Look at this place—" He swiped his hand through the air, taking in the room cluttered with rollers, brushes and pans and painted white from top to bottom including the bars. "And you're threatening to do the same to the library. What's next, the firehouse? White fire engines? And you call me irrational! *That's* irrational.''

"You're the one handing out tickets like Halloween candy.''

"A purple drinking fountain?''

"It's very retro.''

"It's…'' His gaze connected with Red's and he saw a flash of realization in her eyes about the same time the truth dawned on him. He let out a deep breath. "Neither of us have been easy to live with lately. Least the good citizens of Paradise Creek didn't tar and feather us and run us out of town.''

But did they have to lock him up with the very woman he'd been trying to put out his mind?

Red glared at the door. "Okay, we're both to blame for this situation and we should talk and straighten things out, but we need to get out of here first.'' She gave him a sassy grin. "You could have the distinction of being the only sheriff on the Eastern Shore to break out of his own jail. If we find something sharp we can trace it around a block or a brick and it'll pop out.''

"Huh?''

"Or a loose floorboard. We can pry it up. In books—''

"The floor's concrete. What kind of books do you…'' His eyes widened. "Chicken?''

"I'm not a chicken, Clay Mitchell. I'm the one trying to come up with some ideas for escape. They may not be the greatest but they're a start. And you're standing around like a big lump, babbling on about me being—''

"I *smell* chicken." He wiggled his eyebrows. "Fried. And potato salad and chocolate cake."

She took a step back and studied him. "You can smell chocolate cake? All I smell is wet paint and old rags."

"That's because you're not hungry."

"You're always hungry."

"I'm a lousy cook." He sniffed the air. "Mrs. Rowley's chicken. Mabel Farley's chocolate cake. And you're a steamroller with curly hair, but never a chicken. Look for a picnic basket in the cells. I'll take the back room. It's around here somewhere."

"Can't we just get out of here? Aren't you one of those guys who can escape from anywhere with a key and a belt buckle?"

"Later. Let's eat."

She planted her hands on her hips. "You know, just once I'd like to hear, *'Oh, Red, would you pretty-please-with-sugar-on-top help me out here?'* and not order me around like some Supreme Court Judge."

"Find the basket yet?" He headed for the back and felt a brush whiz past his arm.

"You and my father are two of a kind. Cookie-cutter images. Bookends. Frick and Frack. He has a one-track mind just like yours. Only time he knew I was around was when he needed me to coordinate his wardrobe. I swear, the man's color blind. If he weren't my only parent, I wonder if I would have let him order me around so easily.''

''What about the fiancé? Why did you let him order you around?''

''I was still in my *letting people have their way* mode. Then I found that campaign button in my bouquet. My maid of honor must have put it there. It was a wake-up call. I realized I was about to make a huge mistake and had to change or I'd make my whole life one big mistake. I can't find your chicken anywhere. Maybe your sniffer's broken. Why didn't they leave the food where we could find it?''

''If we saw it before they locked us in here we might have suspected there was something afoot.''

She tossed aside a drop cloth and looked behind a ladder leaning against the wall. ''Nothing here but dust bunnies and paint-splattered papers.''

He studied her through the bars. Red's father may be some big important something back in D.C., but if Clay ever ran into him or this ex, there would be words and Clay Mitchell would have the last one. Red didn't deserve being lied to and manipulated.

''If you ordered your ex around like you do me I bet she threw more than a paint brush at you.''

''Elizabeth?''

She looked up. ''How many ex's do you have, Clay Mitchell?''

"One. Just one. And the only thing she ever threw at me were divorce papers, five years ago."

"Irreconcilable bossiness?"

"Too poor, too ordinary, too boring." He searched behind a pile of paint cans and didn't find the basket. "She might have mentioned somewhere I was a little bossy."

"*No.* Did you run after her?"

"Sold our house, paid off the credit cards she'd maxed out and moved back in with Uncle Albert since he'd broken his leg and needed some help. Besides, he's a good cook and doesn't mind that I'm a small-town sheriff—except when I give him a ticket—and he doesn't mind the bossy part."

"Think again, Mr. Congeniality, *that's* why we're locked up in here." She stepped over some newspapers and hunkered down, peering around the floor.

"And you being Picasso's sidekick didn't have anything to do with any of this present predicament?"

"Hey, here's your chicken. And it does smell great." She kicked aside a can and scooted the wicker basket from under the cot.

Clay came up beside her as she stood, basket in hand. He flipped back the red-checkered cloth as his stomach growled and his taste buds went on full alert. "Least they didn't intend to starve us to death." He grinned. "Chow's on."

"Shouldn't we escape first, eat later? Business before pleasure?"

He rested his hand on her shoulder and gazed into her eyes. "The chicken will give you strength for tunneling. We can use the bones to dig."

"You have no imagination, Clay Mitchell. We could rot in here before you'd come up with a way to get us out."

He tipped her chin with his index finger, bringing her face to his. "Getting out's not the problem. What we have to decide on is how to coexist so we don't wind up back in here."

She looked at him with wide eyes that any man could get lost in…especially him, and said, "Albert, Mrs. Rowley, Jake? They'd throw us in jail again?"

"When it comes to upsetting the workings of their town we could rot in this place."

He let her go, trying to forget about her eyes. "You sit on that side." He nodded to the end of the cot. "I'll park on this side."

She cleared her throat and played with a stray curl at her temple. Dang, did she have to do that? He was just getting over the eyes and now he was thinking about her hair. He swallowed and took the basket to keep his hands occupied and out of trouble as she asked, "How—how long do you think we'll be locked up in here, together?"

"Hard to say." They'd eat fast and come up with a solution to live and let live, then get out of here. He concentrated on his craving for food instead of his craving for Red. ''Ah, do you like white meat or dark?''

''Dark. We could be in here quite a while then, huh?'' She nibbled her bottom lip. He wished he were the one doing that nibbling.

''I'm going to wash my hands.'' She nearly ran to the back room. Thanks heavens! A short reprieve from looking at and salivating over Red.

Clay heaped the containers of food on the cot, making a barrier across the middle. No hip-to-hip, shoulder-to-shoulder stuff.

Food. He had to keep his mind on the food and do a better job at it than he had done at Ruth's. He sat down and grabbed a drumstick and took a bite. Thunder suddenly shook the building. Another storm? More rain? Damn, this couldn't be good. The ground was already soaked. What ever happened to October, the dry season?

''Okay,'' she said as she came back into the cell. ''I'm ready.''

She'd washed her face! Well, of course she washed her face, what did he expect? Even under harsh fluorescent lights she was more beautiful than ever. She'd be dazzling in moonlight or candlelight.

He wanted her, dammit. He wanted her more than he'd ever wanted another woman in his life, and the portion of his anatomy right below his belt buckle didn't give a squat that getting involved with her was a really dumb thing to do.

HOPE LOOKED from Clay to the array of food. It was in a straight line, like a barrier. Thank heavens! Being locked up alone with Sheriff Clay Mitchell and keeping her hands and lips and other body parts off of him was asking a lot. Especially since she'd been fantasizing about doing the exact opposite since she left him at Ruth's.

She sat down cross-legged on her end of the cot with her back up to the wall, keeping as far from the too handsome, too virile sheriff as possible. She looked at the food and not him, then helped herself to the potato salad and a fresh roll. She snatched a fork and took a bite. It was the next best thing to…sex.

Why, why, why when she was with Clay was her whole mind set on sex in one form or another? She couldn't even eat potato salad without thinking about it—least, not when Clay was sitting beside her. *Think of something else.* "This salad's incredible, the roll pure heaven."

"You need to be here at our summer fair. Rides, fireworks. In September we do clam bakes."

This was better. They were talking food and fun. Nothing to get her hormones in a twitter. He was just a guy, she was just a gal. She stabbed another forkful of potato salad. "Hey, you took the only drumstick." She leveled a threatening look his way.

"You're going to whine over a drumstick?"

"Told you I was spoiled."

He tore off a piece and held it out toward her and she bit into the chicken.

Big mistake. Not because it wasn't great chicken, but because her lips closed over Clay's fingers.

He seemed to freeze in place as his gaze locked with hers. Passion sparked in his eyes. Her heart drummed in her chest and blood bubbled hot in her veins. The only reason she didn't fall down was because she was already sitting. Clay Mitchell would never be just another guy to her.

Slowly, seductively he pulled his fingers from her lips. She swallowed the chicken in one gulp, then whispered, "Oh boy."

He gave her a tight smile. "Until right now—" he swiped a smear of gravy from her lips "—I thought I was the only one who thought that." His voice was deep and low and arousing.

"You should have let me go to Dover."

"Too late."

"*Oh boy* doesn't change the fact that we're all wrong for each other."

His eyes darkened.

"Except for—" she swallowed "—sex."

His eyes dropped a shade more.

"Just because we feel this attraction doesn't mean all our problems vanish. It just makes them worse."

"What do you want to do, Red?"

Cry from sheer frustration. "Be friends?"

If she'd slapped him upside the head with a dead

mackerel he probably wouldn't have looked more surprised.

"Friends?"

"Well, what did you expect me to say? Let's do
the horizontal hula and to hell with everything else
going on between us?"

The lights flickered, flickered again, then died.

"Horizontal hula?"

She gulped in a big breath. Shew! At least she
didn't have to look at Clay and be turned on and
teased and tempted to do a hula. "It's so dark in here
I can't even see the windows."

Big sigh from across the cot. The kind that went
beyond having the electricity out and suggested there
were far bigger problems than that. "It's a jail, there
aren't any windows. If there were windows you
would have painted over them, and I'm sure being
friends will just solve all of our problems. Solve everything. I'll get an oil lamp. It's on the shelf by the
door."

"Staying away from each other didn't work, so we
have to try something different."

The cot gave way as Clay got up. She listened to
his solid footsteps on the concrete floor followed by
a scrape, then a crash. He groused, "It would be nice
if you put all your painting paraphernalia in one place
instead of strewing it all over creation."

"My stuff isn't in one place because I don't paint
in one place. You're just crabby because we're in this

predicament and now that I think about it, I moved the lamp, a reel of rope and a box of office supplies to the back room. The lamp should be dry by now.''

''Dry? Why was it wet?''

''You don't want to know. I'll get it.''

''Stay put. One of us risking a broken neck is enough.''

She got up from the cot, trying to remember exactly where in the back room she'd put the darn lamp and collided flat into Clay. She knew it was Clay not just because he was the only person with her, but because his broad chest was pressed firmly to hers, his muscular arms steadied her, his strong hands kept her from falling and her heartbeat skyrocketed from being near him. His quick breaths teased her hair and she inhaled his unique male scent.

His voice was a rough whisper when he said, ''I can't do this anymore.''

''But the lamp's just in the—''

''I want you. Here and now. No more dancing around the fact that you are the most beautiful, enticing, sexy woman I've ever met and you excite me to the point of disaster. I want to make love to you more than I've ever wanted to make love before and I don't give a flying fig that it's not what we should do, that we should stay away from each other or that we should be friends. In case you haven't noticed, it's not working.''

Then he lowered his voice and said, "The question is, Red-from-D.C., do you want to make love to me?"

"You—you think I'm beautiful and sexy and... what was the other thing?"

"Enticing."

"Right. I didn't know you thought any of those things about me."

"Well, now you do."

"And you want to make love to me here, in this jail?"

"Or on Main Street, or anyplace else you prefer. I don't care."

"I'll get pregnant."

"That's your only objection?"

"It's a very big objection."

He let out a long sigh, then rested his cheek on her forehead and tenderly kissed the tip of her nose. "You won't get pregnant." His hands slid under her sweatshirt and trailed up her sides. "I have protection."

"Why?"

He stopped dead. "Why? Because... Because..." He framed her face with his palms and looked at her through the darkness. She could tell even though she couldn't see. "Because in case I find a woman who wants to go to bed with me I'm ready, all right?"

"That's a big lie. I don't believe you for one minute. You're not the kind of guy who goes around jumping into bed with any woman who comes along.

And I know you're not that kind of guy because if you were, we wouldn't be standing here in a dark jail cell having this conversation because I wouldn't have anything to do with you.''

He was quiet for second as he took in her words.

''You think you know me pretty well, don't you?''

''Of course I do. If I didn't I wouldn't be standing in a dark—''

''Jail with me. I got the picture.'' He tangled his fingers in her hair and she heard him inhale deeply, appreciatively. ''I've got protection with me because I've hoped, and even dreamed on occasion, that somehow, some way, you and I would make love and I wanted to be ready if it happened. I've wanted this, you and me together, since you crashed into my life. I've never felt this way about a woman, and I never thought you felt this way, too.''

His voice was a whisper as he continued, ''Guess I was wrong.'' He brushed her lips with his, leaving a trail of fire as he went. ''I'm really glad I was wrong.'' His voice had a low deep quality full of want and promise. She really liked the promise part, and Clay Mitchell wanting her was the fulfillment of *her* dreams.

She braced herself in anticipation of what he would do next knowing it would be wonderful, hoping she wouldn't combust. Then his lips claimed hers hard and fast and strong and any hope of avoiding combustion was lost forever. His lips were hot and moist and he pressed them to hers with such passion that her mind whirled and she sagged against him. He supported her in his arms and braced her body against his own, making her feel wanted and cherished and so much a part of him. He buried his face in her neck and his breath heated her sensitive flesh. Her bones went to rubber as he whispered, "You have incredible skin."

"You have incredible everything." She felt him smile against her nape. Then he pulled away from her just a bit and looked down at her, studying her in the darkness. She could feel his gaze on her.

He said, "Maybe—maybe we should go. Just get out of here before we regret what's damn sure to happen."

"*Now* you want to escape? After we've—"

She felt him press a key into her palm and close her fingers around it. "We don't have to escape. I am the sheriff. I have keys to my own jail."

She was torn, she really was. Should she find the lamp and make wild, passionate love to Clay and toss good sense to the wind, or should she find the lamp and beat him over the head with it for keeping them in here all this time? Then again, if he hadn't kept them in here, they wouldn't be where they were right now. Was that a good thing or a bad one? Right now it was difficult to think of making love with Clay Mitchell as a bad thing. Beating him over the head was beginning to lose its appeal.

"Why didn't you let us out before?"

"We really have to figure out how to get along while you're here. That hasn't changed."

His chest rose and fell rapidly against her nipples hard with wanting. His obvious desire for her pushed firmly against her abdomen, making her crazy with anticipation. "I think we found it." She took the key and slipped it into his pocket.

"You sure about this?"

She grinned into the darkness. "A question? From Clay Mitchell? I think this is the first time you've asked my opinion on anything."

She could tell he was smiling again and it was a great smile, the kind that lit up his whole handsome face and the thought of not making love to Clay seemed like the most stupid thought she'd ever had in her entire life.

CLAY KNEW HER DECISION when he felt the full, confident pressure of her moist lips against his as she slid her arms around his neck bringing them closer still. Never before had his self-control disintegrated so swiftly. His desire for Red strained against the confines of his clothes as her kisses became deeper, stronger, more frantic, fueling the fire already raging inside him.

Every muscle in his body was rock-hard. His throat was tight, his breathing ragged. "I want to see you in lamplight," he said. "I want to make love to you slowly, little-by-little, bit-by-bit, at a snail's pace so I can savor every wonderful inch—''

''Too late.'' She nipped his bottom lip, cutting him off. ''No time.'' Her voice was raspy, her breathing erratic. Her fingers frantically tugged on his belt, struggling with the buckle till it came free. His insides blazed at her impatience. He unzipped her jeans letting them slide to the floor in a soft telltale swoosh. Her fingers gently, tenderly stroked his erection. He thought he'd die from the sheer pleasure of her intimate touch.

He sucked in a quick breath through clenched teeth, fighting for the last threads of control that had to be around somewhere before he unraveled completely. ''You are incredible.''

''You're…big.''

He grinned into the darkness as he eased her cotton panties over her hips, reveling in the feel of her wonderful soft skin sliding under his palms. His insides clenched into a tight knot as he eased his finger between her legs, to her most feminine parts. She gasped as her thighs opened for him, letting him feel how wonderful, how desirous of him she truly was. ''You're so hot, so wet, so incredibly perfect, just as I'd imagined.''

He felt her shudder against him. ''I want you now, Clay. Please. Hurry.''

Thunder boomed outside and her plea tore through him like a strike of lightning. Passion slashed at the last bits of his control. He eased his fingers from her, then slid off her panties, letting her step free. His fingers shook as he fumbled in his wallet for the condom and four hands slid it in place. He kissed her, then lifted her, bracing her back against the iron bars. "Wrap your legs around my waist, sweetheart. Easy now. Slow. Relax."

His lips grazed hers as she said, "I don't want to relax. Not now. I want you."

Her breath was hot as it fell across his face. Her words were short and desperate. She gripped his shoulders and locked her legs around his middle bringing him swiftly and completely inside her with one thrust.

His head reeled in surprise and wonder. He heard her gulp in a quick breath. Her grip on his shoulders tightened to a frenzied squeeze and a mind-numbing passion consumed his very being. The sound of his name filled the dark room and echoed off the walls as her climax matched his and they surrendered to an intimacy that would no longer be denied.

CLAY FELT HER HEAD sag onto his shoulder as his heartbeat continued to race. "You're amazing." He kissed her neck, her ear and nuzzled her hair, wanting to taste and feel her again and again. Slowly, reluctantly he let her down, thrilling in the feel of her body sliding over his. "You're an incredible lover."

Her voice was throaty as she said, "I've never been an incredible anything to anyone."

He kissed her eyes, then grazed her lips with his. "I think we've found your niche."

She laughed, then kissed him lightly. He'd never tire of her mouth on his. She said, "Maybe you're wrong. Maybe we should make love again just to make sure."

He could feel his lips smiling against her. "This storm's not letting up. The electric's still off, which means the utility people are up to their armpits in trouble. Jake may need help. As much as I don't want to leave here, we have to go. I've got a bad feeling about all this."

"Wouldn't Jake come get you if there was a problem?" She nipped his chin. "He probably remembers where you are."

"Jake's trying to prove himself but he may need help." He kissed her, memorizing the feel of her lips slightly swollen from his other kisses. "Besides, this is—"

"Your town. I know." She heaved a sigh. "I better get dressed. Paradise Creek isn't ready for my rendition of Lady Godiva."

The thought of Red, naked, on a white horse, made his insides burn like coals on a glowing fire. He trailed his hand over her bare hip, across her smooth back, embracing her, bringing her tight to him. He could feel his heart beating with hers. Then he kissed her, long and hard and deep, and wanting nothing more than for their time together to last forever.

HOPE BUTTONED her jeans and watched Clay come her way with the lighted oil lamp. A soft golden glow surrounded him, giving him a dreamy quality. That's exactly how she felt about him, as if this were all a dream, the sort that didn't happen very often but made a heck of an impression when it did.

Clay asked, "Are you ready to go?" He held up the packed wicker basket and handed it to her. Then he nodded toward the oak door.

She took the basket but she didn't move. "Ready for what, is the question. What are we going to do now, Clay? About you and me and being in here together like…we were? Making love wasn't in either of our plans. We were supposed to discuss our friendship. Some discussion."

Silence loomed between them like a heavy mist, then he said, "Stay in Paradise Creek. We'll work something out."

"You are who you are, Clay. I don't want to live in your shadow or anyone else's."

"Things between us are more complicated now, but we can't behave as if we never made love. And I wouldn't want to."

Her heart swelled. "Neither do I."

He kissed her on the forehead. "Ready to go?"

She put her hand in his. It felt good, so right as if that's how the two of them belonged in life.

He said, "I want you to know that whatever happens out there—" he hitched his chin at the oak door "—I'll never forget this night." He gave a little laugh. "Even though I don't know your name, you'll always be special to me and nothing can change that, no matter who you are or where you're from or what the future holds for us."

He sealed his pledge with a kiss that melted her heart with its sincerity and filled her soul with a profound sense of happiness.

Then Clay unlocked the door and they stepped into the outer office.

Chapter Six

Clay held the lamp high so they could see where they were going. Rain beat hard against the windowpanes. More thunder shook the entire courthouse. He held on to Red's hand tighter as they walked farther into the office. "From the sounds of things outside, I think we should build an ark."

"And leave all bugs behind. 'Course I'll have to shop for cruisewear."

He gently squeezed her hand. He liked having her beside him, sharing her thoughts and pieces of her life. Talking about his divorce and her near-marriage were deeper conversations than he'd had with most people in town. Not that he wanted to go around spilling his guts every time he was with her, but it was a welcome change to have someone interested in him as a person and not just the great problem-solver of Paradise Creek.

He held the lamp high, giving them a little more light. "Good thing we have the lantern to get us through this maze somebody made of my office. I can't imagine doing this in the dark.''

She poked him in the ribs and he chuckled as they stepped over cans and around ladders. ''I'm going to clean it all up very soon. I just got a little carried away and now I need to fix a few things.''

''Like my desk.''

''For starters.''

When he got to his desk, he picked up the phone as Red put the basket of food on his chair. ''Damn, the lines are down.'' He glanced back to the window. ''It must be worse out there than I thought. I wonder where Jake is. I wonder what he's up to.'' His chest tightened. ''I wonder how bad things are....''

Red tried the phone again and when it didn't work, she said, ''Why don't you just use dispatch, he's probably in his cruiser. Or get him on his cell phone?''

He tipped her chin with his index finger, bringing her gaze to his. ''Storms play hell with dispatch reception. And tell me, Red-from-D.C., have you seen any of those big ugly blinking cellular towers around here?''

He stroked her soft lips with his thumb and his blood stirred. He wanted her. Again. Would there ever be a time when he didn't? But there was work to do, so he folded his hands across his chest, instead of folding them around Red. ''We don't have cellular in these parts. Paradise Creek isn't a big customer area.''

"So how do you all keep up with each other around here?" She put her arms around his waist and gazed up at him, making him wonder just how in the world he was supposed to keep his hands to himself and think of work!

"The boats have VHF radios and communicate that way. Onshore, we all seem to meet up at Katie's Kitchen sometime during the day to find out what's going on, or hash out our problems. Instead of cute phones we get fresh coffee and apple pie à la mode."

He watched a smile creep across her face. "You know, I was feeling pretty good about my cell phone until you threw in the pie à la mode."

The lock of the main door suddenly turned and the door swung open. An illuminated cone from a flashlight danced toward them. Only one other person had the key to the office. "Hi, Jake."

The cone stopped. "Clay? How the heck did you get out of... I was just coming to get you. Look, I know you must be mad as a mule chewing bumblebees right about now, and I can understand that, but we've got problems, and they're mighty big ones."

Jake's wet boots slapped against the wood floor as he drew near. "The rain's washing mud and gravel across all the roads on account of the ground's already soaked clear through. Little Creek and the rest are swelled up, looking more like rivers. Worst I've ever seen 'em. The Owens's chicken coop flooded, damn near floated away. I had to help get the hens into the garage. Don't mind telling you that was no fun job and those chickens are none too happy about doing their roosting on a Chevy Nova.''

"What direction is the wind blowing from?"

Jake swiped rain from his face. "Northwest, Clay. Wish I could tell you different, but I can't. The barometer's dropping like a rock. It's cooking up to be a mighty poor night for the Eastern Shore."

Clay went to the window and peered into the darkness. Apprehension ate at his gut as Red asked, "What difference does it make what direction the wind blows from?"

Jake said, "When strong winds come from the northwest they build up the waves on the Bay and they tend to blow the water backwards, up the creeks, making them flood even more than expected."

"The Chesapeake Bay's going to flood?"

"Not the Bay, just the creeks feeding the Bay, and it's only bad when they're full and that's in the springtime when we have runoff and the winds. Everybody knows to keep an eye out in the spring."

Clay cracked his knuckles as he watched fat drops slither down the glass. "But this is October, the dry season, and it's rained more than I can ever remember." He turned from the storm and glanced at the illuminated hands of his watch. "It's nearly ten. People will be turning in for the night, especially since there's no electric for TV or outside lights to see what's going on."

A shudder ripped clear through him as Jake added, "A lot of people will be caught unawares on this one, Clay. They know it's raining but not how much or what the wind's got in store. What are you going to do?"

Good question. And everyone in Paradise Creek would expect him to have answers. Trouble was, he'd never seen weather like this, so he didn't have any answers he knew would work. He'd have to shoot from the hip and hope the rain stopped before things got desperate. "Jake, go ring the bell in the tower. That will alert the town that something's up. Take Red and get Uncle Albert, Carlie and Sam and his crew and evacuate the folks along Little Creek to the school gym. If it floods, they'll be hit first. Keep a roster and make sure everyone's accounted for. No stragglers left behind and no excuses for not following my evacuation orders. We're all coming through this together."

Jake said, "I'll set up lookouts to keep track of the rising water and evacuate Main Street if the water gets there. What are you going to do about the farmers along the creek beds up aways? They sure as heck can't hear the bell and the phones are dead."

"I'll drive out along Willow Pond and warn the folks up there, then double back along the creek to make sure the summer cottages aren't occupied. I'll close the roads if they get washed out by the dry creeks that run across them. There aren't going to be any dry creeks tonight."

He felt Red's hand on his arm. "And I'll go with you. You shouldn't be out there alone."

"You?" Oh boy. Bad answer. Red was bristling like some mistreated porcupine, he was sure of it. But the one person he didn't need along when he went out into this storm was Red. Not only didn't she know one thing about floods, he'd worry himself crazy that something would happen to her. He had enough to worry about right now.

"Yes, me, you big oaf."

He patted her hand. "Jake needs your help."

She swatted his hand away. "Jake will have plenty of help, and I am not some piece of fluff that's only good for... Well, you know what I mean. I can take care of myself, and I *can* help you."

"By what? Getting caught on a rooftop? Screeching if you see a bug? Deciding what colors to paint the detour signs we put up?"

"Nice try, but I'm not falling for your little ploy." She set her hands on her hips. "No matter how hard you work at getting me fighting mad so we'll storm off in opposite directions and you can be on your merry way without me, it's not going to work. I know how you think. I know all your little tricks. I'm here and I'm going with you." She jutted her chin. "And you're going to let me because I'm right and you know it and you can't talk your way out of it."

Clay let out a huge sigh. "Okay, okay. I don't have time to argue, but we have to hurry." He handed her the lantern off the desk and clicked on his flashlight. "We'll need that rope you put in the back room. I'll find you some rain gear, then we've got to get a move on. Things are getting really bad out there."

Satisfaction flashed across her face. "You won't be sorry."

"I'm sure I won't."

Jake said, "Clay, have you lost your ever-loving mind? You can't be serious about Red going out in this—"

"Not to worry, Jake. I'll keep her safe, you know I will." He kissed Red hard on the lips, feeling a little guilty for what he was about to do. Then he watched her head for the oak door they'd come through minutes ago.

He walked to the entrance as Red's lamplight faded deeper into the room. She paused, then turned and faced him. Even though darkness separated them, their gazes locked the split second before she yelled, "No!" and Clay slammed closed the heavy oak door, locking her safely on the other side and out of harms way.

"I'm going to strangle you with my bare hands, Clay Mitchell! Let me out of here right now! You can't do this to me."

Red's banging on the door, mixed with her threats and accusations about him being a son of questionable parentage, was louder than the thunder overhead. He turned his attention to Jake and tried to ignore the din. "Whatever you do, don't let her out unless you absolutely have to. She's just stubborn enough to try and find me, and if there's one thing I don't need tonight is to baby-sit Red."

"I heard that, you creep," came the voice from the other side of the door. "You just wait till I get out of here, Clay Mitchell."

He grimaced. She was madder than a wet hen and getting madder by the minute. He continued talking to Jake. "I'll leave this key in the lock so you or someone else can open it in a hurry if things reach the crisis stage and you have to get to her fast. We don't know when this rain is going to stop or how much flooding we're going to get."

Jake ran his hand over his face. "I should go see about the creeks, Clay. Not you. You need to stay here and coordinate things. Everyone trusts your judgment and will do what you tell them."

"Are you kidding? If the flood gets really bad and we have to let Red out, I don't want to be within five miles of this place." He shared a grin with Jake, then rested his hand on Jake's shoulder. "Besides, you co-ordinate just fine."

Clay hoped he sounded more confident than he felt. Not that Jake wasn't a good deputy, but this was Clay's town. His responsibility. Unfortunately, he couldn't be in two places at once. "I'm not risking anybody's neck in this mess but my own. It's my job.'' He arched his left brow. "That's why they pay me the big bucks, remember?" They both laughed.

Red's pounding on the door continued as Clay snatched his flashlight, then grabbed his rain gear from the rack. Jake nodded at the oak door and said, "You'll have to face her sooner or later, Clay, and it ain't going to be pretty." He pushed back his yellow rain hat and grinned. "And I bet it'll make this dang storm seem like a puny drizzle."

TWO HOURS LATER Hope stepped on the brakes of the Ford Bronco she'd borrowed from Carlie Lewis and rounded Willow Pond. Pond? Ha! She skirted the rising water as rain pelted the windshield, making visibility a real challenge.

Like she needed another challenge tonight. Wasn't escaping from jail enough of a challenge? Then she laughed out loud, feeling very smug because she had, indeed, done just that. And she hadn't resorted to dynamiting or digging. She didn't have to since that star Clay had given her was in her pocket. All she had to do was straighten out the pin on the back, stick the star into the lock and push out the key on the other side, letting it fall onto a paper she'd shoved under the door. When she pulled the paper back, there was the key. 'Course she could have used a screwdriver or some other tool to push out the key but using the star held a certain sense of revenge that made her feel warm and fuzzy all over.

Dang, she was good! Actually, it was Nancy Drew who was good. Which story had she used that key trick in, anyway?

Wind blasted the car and Hope shivered in the rain gear she'd also borrowed from Carlie, and gripped the steering wheel tighter as the car rounded the next curve. No cruiser here. Where was Sheriff Clay Mitchell? When he was talking to Jake in the office, Clay said he'd be heading up this way, so where in blazes was he? He should have doubled back by now. She carefully headed down a dip in the road, keeping an eye out for the cruiser.

Clay would be furious when she caught up with him, but she wasn't about to let the man she'd just made mad passionate love with get washed away in a flood without anyone around to help. 'Course his crack about baby-sitting her coupled with the way he'd tricked her into that jail made her all the more determined to find his lordship and tell him exactly what she thought of him and what he had done.

Hope Stevens was her own woman now, doing what *she* wanted to do and Sheriff Clay Mitchell better get used to the idea that she was a very capable woman and could handle any situation just fine, thank you very much. She straightened her spine as she rounded another bend, looked for Clay, and drove straight into a torrent of angry water, making a huge splash that washed over the hood of the Bronco, stopping it dead and killing the engine.

Huh? What was water doing here? This was a road. Roads didn't just end, they went somewhere, but not into a river. She looked in her rearview mirror, catching a glimpse of the road she'd driven over, and she looked forward to the road coming out of the water. She tried to start the car, but there were no comforting engine sounds.

Electrical failure? But the wipers and lights worked. Well it was some kind of failure because the Bronco just sat there like a big metal island as water streamed around it.

She opened the door and the wind tried to yank it from her hand. Even in the darkness she could make out the muddy water swirling inches below the doorframe. The car suddenly lurched. It was turning around all by itself! It was floating. She grabbed the steering wheel. Oh yeah, that would do a lot of good. Then the Bronco teetered front-to-back. Water lapped inside.

She was not going to drown! She refused. She could just hear Clay saying ''I told you so'' over her coffin. And he wouldn't remember the chocolate Spiegel suit at all. He'd bury her in denim because she sneaked out of his jail.

Mustering all her courage, she stepped down into the water. It whirled around her thighs, numbing her legs. Wind snapped her jacket and her hair whipped her face. She stepped away from the car so she wouldn't be carried along with it if it floated away completely. Now she owed Carlie a new Bronco and Delia a van. Life was not getting simpler.

The water was shallower now. She took another step. It was shallower still. The shore was only a few feet away. She could make it. She'd be fine. No "I told you so," and no denim. Relief poured over her, giving her confidence, until a sudden surge of water hit her broadside, sweeping her off her feet. Terrified, panicked, she gasped and kicked to regain her footing, but was thrown on her back, then tugged along by the current.

CLAY GOT OUT of his cruiser and turned his collar against the wind and rain. His headlights reflected ominously in the water flowing across the roadway. Another dry creek that was anything but dry. He dragged a fallen tree limb from the side to block the road and keep some unsuspecting driver from winding up in a real mess. He lugged another limb and added it to the first, then tied on a section of yellow Caution tape to make it look like an official barricade and not just a fallen— Damn, was that a car floating by?

He took the flashlight from his side pocket and clicked it on, illuminating the churning water. It was a Ford Bronco. Black. Carlie Lewis's? Was she delivering medication out this way? Was she trapped inside? Hell! Clay aimed his light at the windshield but only got a reflection off the glass. He ran down the side of the creek, following the car. "Carlie?" He hung out on a tree limb and aimed the flashlight again. He didn't see anyone but still called, "Carlie? Are you—"

The limb creaked, and Clay jumped back to solid ground. That was close. The last place he wanted to be was in the middle of that torrent of muddy—

The ground under him suddenly gave way and he stumbled backwards. He fought to regain his balance, snagged a branch, then it snapped and he landed back-side-first into the water. He was submerged for a moment, then fought his way up. He gasped, filling his lungs with air as the flood swished him along. He couldn't get his footing because of the slippery, uneven bottom. He dodged a rock, was swept around a bend, then smacked into a fallen tree trunk. "Umph!"

Least the tree wasn't moving. He held on to it. It seemed to be caught on another pile of driftwood that had collected on the outside of the bend. But it wouldn't hold for long—the water seemed to be picking up speed as the wind died, and it would work the pile loose in no time. His feet touched bottom, giving him a moment of stability. He snagged his arm around another log higher on the pile and pulled himself up till only his legs were in the water.

Relief ran through him. Thank heavens Red wasn't here. The only thing that could make his situation worse was to have her in this mess. He reached again, but his hands connected with something that didn't feel like a log at all. It felt more like cloth. An ear-piercing scream filled the air and his fingers were whacked hard. Ouch! Damn!

Someone was up there! Someone was trapped on the woodpile like he was! He yanked his hand back, but there were more whacking sounds, like wood against wood, along with, "Die, bug, die."

He froze. No! No, flipping way! Then he thought of all the other unlikely places where Red had un-expectedly turned up.

"Red?"

The whacking stopped. "C-Clay?"

He levered himself, coming face-to-face with her. She was speechless for a moment, so that gave him a chance to say, "What the hell are you doing out here in the middle of nowhere with Carlie Lewis's car and—"

"See! See!" she said in a high-pitched squeaky voice that was nothing like her usual voice as she wagged a log at him. Her eyes were fully dilated, her arms shaking as she said, "I told you not to come out here alone, that there could be trouble and there wouldn't be anyone to help you, but did you listen to me, did you? No! So I followed you and now we're both—"

"Put down the log." She wasn't rational. Heck, he wasn't much better. A guaranteed by-product of a near drowning. He felt the pile of wood shift. Oh, dang! "Look, we have to get out of here, now! Later we can argue about us both being out here. This mound we're perched on is getting ready to wash away and take us along with it."

Her eyes were wild and her voice shook as she said, "Where can we go? I can't see anything. You can't see anything, either. How can we leave here when we don't know where we're going?"

"We'll head away from the sound of the water." *And hope like hell there's land on the other side of this heap.* He gingerly climbed up beside her and pushed on a huge tree trunk that was part of their temporary peninsula. The tree was leaning up, away from the water. It seemed solid, and right now that was a very good thing indeed. "Follow me."

"I can't do this, Clay." She shook her head. "I don't know how? I can't even guess how. I'm staying here with the logs."

The pile shifted again. He and Red were out of time. "You're right. You just stay put, and I'll get help. But try not to fall through the cracks, okay. We're pretty high up here."

"High?"

"And if you do fall, be real careful because way down there is where the big black water bugs live."

She bit her lip as she peered down into the dark abyss. She looked back at him for a split second, then hugged the tree trunk next to her, hooked her leg around it and scooted on. Without even bothering to look back to him she tested the next log to make sure it held, then wiggled onto it. She reached again and stopped. "Grass! Clay, I touched grass! It's just over this tree."

She turned to him, her grin white against the black night. Then he crawled behind her, following her onto solid ground. They were huffing, panting and cold to the bone as the rain beat down, slapping against their wet clothes and the soaked earth. He wrapped his arms around her and she buried her face in his neck and said, "There aren't any black bugs down there, are there?"

"Nah." He smoothed her hair back and kissed her cheek. "The snakes eat them."

She made little dismal whiny sounds. "I'm pathetic."

He tipped her chin with his fingers and kissed her, tasting the rain on her lips. Never had rain tasted so sweet. "If you were pathetic you would have drowned. You never would have made it here and managed to save yourself in this mess. You're brave and strong and incredibly beautiful. But aren't you just a little sorry you didn't stay in jail?"

"No!" She sniffed. "Maybe." She pulled in a breath. "How'd the pioneers do it? How'd they find places like Paradise Creek and build it?"

"One step at a time. We've got to get to town. Carlie's SUV has probably floated far away by now and my cruiser's back around the bend. The rain hasn't stopped but the winds have slacked off. We're not getting blasted as hard and the water's racing downstream like mad.''

"That's good, isn't it? The streams aren't flooding like they were before.'' He felt her shiver.

"Yes, but it's bad because all the pent-up water that was held in check before is now heading right for the south end of Paradise Creek.'' He took her hand. ''Let's get out of here. Least we're on the same side of the creek as the cruiser. We don't have to go back across.''

He looked at the racing water, taking everything in its path to the Bay. ''Come on. Just don't get too close to the water, it's washing the ground away as it comes up. That's how I ended up here.''

"I drove.''

She had his hand in a death grip as they slogged through weeds and underbrush. He said, ''Least we can't get any wetter.''

"I'll try and remember that as a good thing.''

They climbed over a fallen tree. Their feet tangled in wet vines. He caught her when she stumbled. Then she caught him.

He stopped and pointed. ''The cruiser's headlights are up ahead. We're almost there.''

Her head sagged against his arm. ''We're going to make it, aren't we.'' It was a statement more than a question and that was good. He boosted her over another tree.

"Wonder where the Bronco is."

He climbed behind her. "The Bahamas."

"Should have stayed with the Bronco." She stopped dead and pointed. "Clay, there's another creek, between us and the cruiser. I can hear it." She took a step back. "How are we going to get over it?"

He took her arm, not letting her retreat farther. "It's not as big as Little Creek. It's just a spring."

She gave him a pointed look. Even in the darkness he could tell she wasn't buying it.

"It's a big spring. We'll hold on to each other and get across."

"We'll drown together."

"We'll make a human chain. I'll tether you across, you'll pull me." He studied her for a moment. She was shivering and scared and near exhaustion. "Can you do that?"

She nodded, a tight little smile at her lips. He kissed her. She was an incredible woman. He was sure she'd never been through anything like this— like he had?—yet she wasn't in a fit of hysterics or whining or crying. His glamour gal from D.C. had a lot of grit.

He led her down toward the creek. The sound of the rushing water getting closer. The headlights from the cruiser offered a little help and he searched for a narrow spot. He found a tree that was still solid in the ground and took off his belt and looped it around the trunk. "I'm going to hold on to this and get you to that rock in the middle." He nodded toward the stream.

"No. No rocks in the water."

"It's not that deep, you can stand. The danger is getting knocked off your feet."

"That's not consoling."

"Then you get to that next rock. See there? Then you can get to shore. It's like connect the dots. Just keep a tight grip on me till you get your footing."

He held on to the belt and Red. She held on to him, then made it to the first rock. Then the next one, then to the shore.

She scrambled onto the ground and when she turned around, he was right behind her. "You followed me?"

"Hell, yes. Think I'm going across this mess first when I've got Daniel Boone here to show me the way?" She leaned against him for a moment. "Seems one of us is always following the other around."

"Let's go home."

"I like the way you say that." He kissed her hair. "And we'd better hurry, Paradise Creek's going to be needing all the help we can give her right now. This night's far from over, Red."

TWENTY MINUTES LATER when Clay reached the sheriff's office after dropping Red off at The Gray, he knew he'd been right about Paradise Creek needing help. A miracle would be better. Water covered all the roads and more electric and phone lines were down than up.

Mrs. Rowley wasn't home, and no one was at the office. He hadn't seen a soul since he reached town, and with all the lights out Paradise Creek reminded him of one of those sci-fi flicks where everyone's been evaporated or beamed up somewhere and there was only one person left on earth. Except this time it would be two, he and Red. Now that could be very interesting, indeed.

He quickly changed into dry clothes and got back in the cruiser. The water was deeper across the roads than when he came into town. He headed for Main Street to check on conditions there. Maybe the flooding wasn't as bad there as he feared it might be. Maybe everyone was at Katie's Kitchen celebrating. Maybe he should give up being sheriff and write fairy tales.

As Clay swung around the corner, the headlights of his cruiser picked out Sam perched on his backhoe, dumping a load of sand in front of Katie's Kitchen. Cars were parked perpendicular to the street with headlights on, illuminating a sandbag brigade. He recognized each and every person working furiously to save Paradise Creek. Kids, parents, grandparents, great-grandparents. People born and raised in this town as well as the come-heres. One line held the large grain bags from the feed store, some even used plastic garbage bags, while the next line filled it with sand and handed it off to someone in the third line to stack.

He watched Mabel Farley hold a bag as Bobby filled it with a shovel of sand. Mrs. Rowley had the same teamwork going with Tommy. Willa Jenkins and Ruth Owens were even working side-by-side, holding and filling, and Uncle Albert was in the stacking line.

The sandbags stood about three feet high and bisected Main Street. The white barricade disappeared between Katie's Kitchen and Something's Fishy. That meant anything below the sandbags was already flooded.

How could this happen? Why couldn't he help this town now, when they needed helping more than ever? He'd never felt this desperate, not even when he'd run away from home so many years ago. This time it wasn't just him in a jam with no way out. There was an entire town at stake. He owed so much to these people and he didn't know how to help them.

He couldn't make it stop raining, or stop the creeks from flowing or move Paradise Creek to higher ground. He couldn't make the sandbags fill faster and get in place quicker. The term *heartache* never had much meaning for him. Until now.

Leaving the lights on, he got out of the cruiser and jogged toward the brigade of sandbaggers. It was more like running in the surf than down Main Street, except there was rain and mud instead of soft sand and waves and sunshine.

He reached the first line of the brigade, stopped beside Tommy and noogied his head.

"Hi, Sheriff Clay. It sure is raining a lot out here, isn't it?"

Clay pulled Tommy's hat farther down on his head to keep the rain off his face. "Got that right, sport." He said to Mrs. Rowley, "I'll take your place. Go sit down. You shouldn't be out here with your heart condition." He turned her collar up around her neck and zipped her rain jacket the rest of the way up.

"Well, bless my soul, if it isn't Clay Mitchell. Guess you think you can show up and start with the orders just because everyone in town was worried about you. Well, you can just forget about me going anywhere because it'll be a lot harder on my heart if we lose this here town than if I hold open a bag or two. Now go grab yourself a bag and start shoveling."

Clay grinned at Tommy and grabbed one of the white bags. He quietly asked Mrs. Rowley, "Are there any casualties or…fatalities?" The word stuck in his throat like a wad of cotton.

"Jake almost broke his arm trying to rescue my Goldie off a floating log. I feel real bad about that, but at least Goldie's safe and sound. Jake's over at

Doc's now, making sure it's okay. You going to put sand in that bag or just hold it all night?''

Clay picked up a shovel as Mrs. Rowley added, ''Heard you locked up Red in that jail of yours. Bet she's fit to be tied.''

''Oh, I sure am.'' It was Red's voice. ''And when this is all over someone's going to pay.''

Clay turned and saw her right behind him as she said, ''If we run out of sandbags, I say we add Sheriff Mitchell's carcass to the heap.''

She winked at Mrs. Rowley and Tommy and offered them a hot drink from the thermos she carried. ''That'll make him good for something.''

Hey, he was good for a lot of things, and right now all of them had to do with Red. How could she forget that he was good at making love to her, teasing her, holding her close. Then she snatched the bag from Clay's hand, reminding him that all those things weren't going to happen any time soon and Paradise Creek needed his full attention.

She said, ''Jake wants to see you. He's over by the backhoe.''

They exchanged looks as he asked, ''I'm guessing it's not good news.''

Her smile died. She pulled in a deep breath and bit her bottom lip. ''No, it's not.''

There was an ominous look in her eyes that he'd never seen before, not even when he met up with her on the pile of logs or when they fought their way to the cruiser. "We didn't lose anyone, did we?"

She shook he head again. "Not that, but the water's coming faster than we thought it would. Jake wants to know what we should do. It's your call."

He glanced at the sandbag line. Rain fell in sheets. He didn't have to talk to Jake to know things were bad, that Paradise Creek was in dire straights. What else could Jake possibly tell him? Was there something that would make their situation even worse? There couldn't be.

Could there?

He gave Red a quick kiss. "I want you to take care of yourself. Promise me that, okay?"

"Only if you do the same."

He looked at her for a long moment, taking in her loveliness and realizing how much he cared for her, and she for him. When this was all over they had to figure things out. They'd been through too much now to simply walk away.

He turned and headed toward the backhoe.

Chapter Seven

Clay swiped rain from his face and sloshed through water as he made his way toward Jake, who was draped in a black, hooded rain jacket. His good arm cradled his bad one in a sling and his face was drawn into hard lines. Clay said, "You just did this to get a little sympathy from Carlie, didn't you."

"Not exactly." Jake flashed a sheepish grin. "Sure glad to see you. Sorry about Red getting out of jail like she did. She was heading out of town before I even knew she was free. How'd she pull off the great escape, anyway?"

"Beats the heck out of me, and I doubt she'll ever share her little secret with us. Probably torture us with it forever. How're you feeling?"

"Been better. Been worse, just can't remember when." He rubbed his chin. "Weather report says the rain's not letting up till at least dawn, Clay. That's five more hours of this stuff." He kicked at a puddle that was quickly becoming a shallow lake. "The wind's dying, creeks are going to flow faster than ever.''

Jake glanced at the white line of sandbags and the people working to make the pile higher. His voice turned gritty. ''Dammit, Clay, it's not going to hold. You know that as well as I do.''

''Yeah.'' He could barely speak and he swallowed hard. ''Main Street and everything south of the court-house is going to get swamped. Maybe worse.'' He managed a brief lopsided grin. ''I told Red we needed to build an ark. Think she'd listen? Hell, no.''

He watched rain drip off the brim of his hat and slither down the front of his yellow rain jacket, taking his grin right along with it. ''This place is ripe for a flash flood when the wind dies out.'' He looked at his watch. ''I'd say we have less than an hour before things get real ugly around here. We'd better be getting everyone to higher ground.''

''And where the heck would that happen to be? The school's already filled with kids and the older folks. The churches can take on some, but they're not all that big.'' He looked down at the hated water. ''We have to come up with something quick. Dang it! We're flooding already.''

Clay glanced at the water now covering the top of his boots. His heart felt like a rock in his chest. ''First thing is for you to tell Sam to get his backhoe out of here before it sinks into the mud. We'll need his equipment later when we clean up. Somehow I'll get everyone organized and out of here.''

"Try a cattle prod. That's the only way they'll leave. This is their town. They're not going to just walk away from it.''

"You find Sam. I'll think of something.'' Though he couldn't imagine what that was.

He ran to his cruiser, his boots splashing every step of the way. He opened the trunk and took out a bullhorn, clicked it on, then scrambled on to the top of the cruiser and stood. His wet pants were plastered to his legs. Rain dripped down the back of his neck and drenched his back. He shivered, as much from the cold as the circumstances. "Everyone listen up. The wind's dying, and the water's coming up fast because the creeks are flowing hard and the current is getting nasty. Main Street's going to get flooded and there's nothing we can do to stop it. The sandbags aren't going to hold. Everyone has to get out of town and move to higher ground. All those who live north of the courthouse need to take in a family who lives south of the courthouse.''

For a second there was a dead silence. No one moved as the rain fell. They all stared at him, frozen by loyalty to the town they loved and weren't ready to lose. Someone yelled, "We can fight this, Clay. We can win. We can't give up. We've had floods before.''

Clay felt a flash of raw fear cut right through him.

He took off his hat and glared down at the crowd. He assumed his most sheriff-like stance. "Now you all listen to me. I'm the sheriff around here and you do what I damn well tell you to do. The water's going to come fast and furious. Get out of town right now and take the person next to you along to make sure no one gets left behind."

The crowd stirred but didn't budge. Clay added, "Anyone who is in this street in five minutes is answering to me personally. Got that! Now move!"

He'd been barking orders in Paradise Creek for ten years now. Would the people do as he said this time, or stay and try for the impossible and maybe lose their lives? He looked over the crowd. How could he save them? Dammit! Why wouldn't they move? What the hell was he going to do? They were just standing there!

Then he saw Red hook Mrs. Rowley's arm through hers and start walking away from the sandbags and up Main Street. Huh? Red, who'd never done anything he told her to do since the day she landed in Paradise Creek, was following his orders now? He blinked a few times to clear his vision, not quite believing what he saw until Uncle Albert hooked arms with Mabel Farley and the two of them followed. Tommy and Bobby and their parents joined the procession, and the rest fell in step. Cars started up, neighbors offered neighbors rides, shelter, food, hugs. Lots of hugs. And tears.

Somehow he'd gotten the people he cared about most in this world to safety. And he'd done it with Red's help. In fact, if it wasn't for her he'd probably still be yammering into that damn bullhorn trying to get everyone to move their stubborn hides and not having any luck at all. Red might drive him nuts and never—well, mostly never—listen to him, but she was one of the best things that had ever come his way. And, tonight, she'd proved it.

Clay stayed where he was, partly to make sure no one lingered behind and partly because he just didn't have the energy to get the hell down. He watched until the last car pulled away and Main Street lay deserted as a graveyard at midnight. Darkness closed in around him, the only light coming from his car. The only sound…the rain.

He was really getting to hate that sound. And he suspected he'd come to hate it a lot more by morning when he saw the damage it did. How was he going to get everyone back in their homes, so they could get on with their lives? How was he ever going to make things right in his town? How could this happen to *his* town?

HOPE TRIED TO GET comfortable on the narrow wooden seat of the rowboat as Clay paddled it down Main Street. Early morning sunshine and clear skies suggesting a normal day in Paradise Creek. The muddy water and deserted buildings that looked more like islands than businesses said things weren't normal at all. A log floated by, reminding Hope of being stranded on the woodpile the night before. She was lucky to be alive and probably wouldn't be if Clay hadn't happened along and saved her.

She poured a cup of coffee to ward off the chill as a green wicker chair bobbed along in the wake of the log. "I know that chair. I think it's from Mabel Farley's backyard, the one that sits under the oak tree. Let's get it."

Clay gave her a disbelieving look. "You've got to be kidding. There's no room in this little boat for that chair."

"That's what you said about me and I'm here."

"Against my better judgment."

"You don't have to be so darn cranky about it. I'm not going to cause any problems. I'm just sitting here, minding my own business."

"So tell me, why does that always end up being my business, too?"

"Let's snag that chair and hang it over somebody's front porch to dry out. Mrs. Farley will appreciate the effort, don't you think?"

"It's one chair."

"It's a start, Clay."

He looked to her and her eyes met his. He stopped rowing for a moment, then nodded. "You're right."

He turned the boat and followed the half-submerged chair past Something's Fishy with its front porch sagging like a wilted flower.

Hope mentally shuddered at the sight of so many neatly maintained buildings now rooted in dirty brown water. She didn't want to give Clay something else to remind him of how bad things were when he could see it for himself at every turn. She was worried about the people who'd lost so much, worried about the town that had to be put back together, worried about the future of Paradise Creek. But, most of all, she was worried about Sheriff Clay Mitchell.

He was the one holding this town together, but who was holding him together?

All night people had come to him at the high-school gym, wanting answers when there weren't any and hoping for words of encouragement. She'd fallen asleep on a bleacher at around two, but Clay hadn't slept at all.

She put down her coffee and reached out toward the chair. "Can you get a little closer? We're almost there, and… I got the leg." She gave a tug. "It must weigh a ton."

"Waterlogged. Don't let it pull you out of the boat. You hang on to it and I'll go slow till we get to Fishy's. We'll loop it onto the good part of the porch."

She glanced at Clay out of the corner of her eye as he aimed for the bait shop. He didn't sit quite as straight today as he usually did, and his eyes weren't the bright clear blue she was used to. He was tired—tired to the bone—and she couldn't think of any way to help him. All she could do right now was not add to his problems and try to be a little optimistic.

She looked around and rolled her eyes. Optimistic? Even a little? About what? There had to be something. "Paradise Creek could do with a nice boutique, don't you think?"

"Sure would make my day." Was that a hint of a smile?

"At least it's not raining."

"How can you tell? Everything's so damn wet I think we'll all grow mold before noon." He stopped rowing and let the boat come to a rest against the side of Fishy's. He grabbed the legs of the chair, hoisted it up and across the boat, then hooked it on to the roof. "That'll hold it till the water goes down. It should dry out some by then."

She figured Clay was about fifty times stronger than she was to have yanked that chair out of the water like he did. Even dead-tired and scruffy, he was very manly, very virile, appealing, remarkably handsome.

He flashed her a little smile this time and her breath caught. Hey, she did it. She got him to smile!

Then her heart somersaulted. She might have gotten Clay to smile, but now she was turned on. How could she think about handsome and get turned on when things were in such a rotten state? At least it was optimistic.

The little boat glided past the front of Katie's Kitchen. Hope's eyes were level with the doorknob, as she said, "There's a piece of the courthouse flag caught on the knob. Can you get me closer? That flag's been through a lot." She unwound the tattered red and white swatch and stuffed it in her pocket. "Guess the water's up about two feet in there, just enough to ruin the refrigeration. All those great crab cakes are fish food by now. Breaks the heart." That was not optimistic. "I'm sure the fish truly enjoyed them."

He gave her a look that suggested her brain was waterlogged right along with everything else.

"You shouldn't be out here, you know. It's too dangerous."

She resisted the urge to deliver her *I can do as I want* speech and went for, "It's nothing like yesterday. There's no current to get caught in, and it's looking like a nice sunny day. There's no traffic, and I've never been in a rowboat before. Besides, everyone else in town is busy taking care of families and property or trying to persuade some generator to run. You shouldn't be out here alone on this reconnaissance mission, and there's no working jail at the moment to keep me from coming along. So, ta-da, here I am. Want me to paddle for a while?"

"It's row. You're sitting in a rowboat. And you're

too damn cheery. This is a wailing-and-gnashing-of-teeth situation, in case you haven't noticed.''

''Well I can't wail and gnash worth beans.'' She handed him the coffee and his fingers grazed hers. Her heart suddenly beat faster and her mouth went completely dry.

Oh boy. One innocent unintentional touch from Clay and she was ready to jump his bones. How could she feel that way when the whole world around them was in a shambles? Then her gaze collided with Clay's and she doubted if there would ever be anything innocent between them again. They had a certain attraction, a special closeness. There was also mind-boggling, hot steamy sex to consider.

''There's something I need to know.''

Yes, yes, yes I'll make love to you here and now in this boat.

''Why did you walk away from the sandbags last night? I'm grateful, don't get me wrong, because you walking away got everyone else going. I just don't understand why you did it.''

So much for making love. Too bad he didn't want to show his gratitude in a more physical way.

He handed her back the coffee, then pulled on the oars again, sending the boat farther down Main Street. She wished he didn't have on a jacket. It would be nice to see Clay's muscles in action. He had great muscles. He had really wonderful action. She swallowed hard, thinking about the last time she experienced that action.

No doubt about it, she was demented. Gone was any trace of the mature, levelheaded woman she was striving to be. She was in the middle of devastation and mayhem and all she could think about was going to bed—or boat—with Clay.

"Red? Are you listening?"

"I can't swim."

"That's why you left last night?"

"And I didn't want to be buried in denim, and I know with all the commotion going on you'd never remember the suit."

"What suit?"

"See, I knew it. That's exactly my point." She leaned forward and chucked him under the chin because it might cheer him a bit and also because she wanted to feel his unshaven face, just the way it would be if they'd awoken together.

She said, "I'm kidding. I really do know how to swim." He was warm and rough and sexy as hell. All this was very very optimistic. "I didn't want to spend any more time in the water. One ride down the Paradise Creek log flume was enough and I doubted that anyone in town wanted to experience an adventure like that."

"In other words, you thought I was right?"

The sun shimmered off tin rooftops and windowpanes. It was warm and invigorating and hinted things would get better. Sunlight glistened in Clay's mussed hair. She touched the thin scar at his lip and the one at his temple. She stroked his cheek, letting the first hint of beard scratch across her fingers. Her insides ached. Her hormones heated to a boil, she felt incredibly optimistic all over. "Yes, you were right, we had to leave."

The boat drifted to the far side of the drugstore and Clay parked the oars along the side of the boat. "Are you coming on to me?"

"What? No. No way." She snapped her hand away from his face and bolted straight up. "This is not the time or place for something like that." She blushed. She could feel the heat sliding up her neck. "Maybe a little."

"You want to make love in a rowboat?"

She swallowed. "The thought did cross my mind for a second or two. It's not that I don't care about all the problems around us, but it would make us feel better and that's good. It would be kind of optimistic, and we could do with a little optimism right now. Besides, last time it was your idea to make love in jail. A rowboat's not any worse than a jail."

He ran his hands over his face and chuckled.

"Don't you dare laugh at me, Clay Mitchell." Though deep down she was glad to hear him laugh.

He leaned forward, and brushed his lips against hers. "I wouldn't think of laughing at you. You brighten my day, Red-from-D.C., and right now that takes a hell of a lot.''

Then he kissed her hard, covering her mouth, his tongue suggesting what her insides were begging him to do. She pulled back just a bit and asked, ''You really think this is a good idea, then?''

He answered by claiming her lips in a fierce kiss as his hands slid under her jacket, then under her sweater. He cupped her breast, making her dizzy. Her fingertips memorized the contours of his face, the roughness of his cheeks, the firmness of his jaw. His hands moved to her waist, then he undid her jeans. She followed his lead and undid his belt and kicked off her shoes. Suddenly, she stopped and said, ''What if somebody comes?''

He tore off his jacket. ''They won't. Like you said, everybody's too busy with other stuff.'' His voice was unsteady as he wrapped his arms around her middle. She reveled in the way he held her as she leaned back onto his jacket. He pulled off her jeans and she felt his gaze on her, studying every inch of her as it came into view. ''You are incredibly beautiful.'' His voice was soft, appreciative, almost worshipful.

His scrutiny should have made her uncomfortable, but it was an incredible turn-on that someone as gorgeous and brave and honorable as Clay Mitchell wanted her so completely. He fumbled in his wallet, found the little blue packet he needed, then protected her.

Whoa, he was big. Her eyes widened. Yesterday she only felt him being big, but today…well, today there was light. Her insides burned for him. Her heart raced. She really liked…the light. She wanted him hard and hot, his flesh to hers. Desire rushed through her like molten lava, and she opened her arms and body to him.

His gaze fell over her like a lover's caress. "I am so glad you wrecked your van in Paradise Creek." He braced himself against the bottom and she watched erotic pleasure burn in his eyes as he slid into her, making love to her, filling her body and her heart. He kissed her eyes and the tip of her nose. "You're incredible, stunning." His lips smiled against hers. "And you're adventurous. And innovative. Very innovated."

She nipped his chin, his stubble rubbing against her tongue as she tasted him. His heat, his scent, his desire invaded every part of her and she never wanted it to end.

HE LOOKED DOWN AT HER, loving the way the reds and golds of her hair caught the sunlight. He watched her dark eyes fill with wanting, then blatant hunger as he slowly moved inside her, letting her lovely body adjust to his. "What can I do to make it better for you?"

"We need to try a bed sometime." Her voice was husky, breathless. She smiled up at him, then locked her legs around his back, her eyes dilating as he filled her completely. He moved again, faster.

"Clay, we're going to upset the boat."

"We'll die happy." He watched her climax build with his own. A sweet agony filled him, making him summon every ounce of self-control till her passion matched his. Fire sparked in her eyes as she gripped his shoulders. Then she yelled his name, hurling them into an explosive private dry world of their own.

He cuddled her against him for a long moment, feeling her breathing return to normal as his did the same. She looked up at him, her eyes bright, her cheeks pink. He said, "You're fantastic, you know that? And you're a screamer."

"Is that a good thing or a bad thing?" Her eyes turned soft and dreamy.

"Good. Very, very good." He kissed her again, knowing he'd never be able to kiss her or make love to her enough. He thought of what she'd been through and the current state of the town and was amazed she lasted this long in Paradise Creek without looking for a quick way out.

She suddenly pushed at him. "Get up. Someone's coming."

"Unless they're walking on water…"

"It's a motorboat. Listen."

"Dang." He struggled to an upright position pulling her after him. He picked up her jeans, underwear and shoes and held them in one hand. He grinned. ''Memorabilia.''

''Give me that.'' She snatched the articles away and swatted at his hand. The distinctive hum of an outboard motor was louder now as she jammed on her shoes.

''Jeans first, sweetheart.''

''Oh, cripes.'' She kicked off the shoes, one landing in the water. She ignored it and quickly pulled on her panties, then her jeans and got back onto the wooden seat.

He straightened his own clothing as Uncle Albert and his motorboat came around the far end of the drugstore. Uncle Albert said, ''I got worried about you two out here all alone. Afraid you might have tipped over or had a problem with the current or debris floating about. I saw Mabel Farley's wicker chair hanging from Fishy's roof. Flood art.''

Clay ran his hand through his hair. ''The water's receded a couple of inches since we came out. It's down a lot from last night. Main Street should be dry by afternoon.''

''Sam's got his generator working and his TV hooked up. When I left he was checking on conditions up and down the Eastern Shore. What we need are some of those big high-pressure hoses to get the mud off everything. And we sure could do with fresh water.'' Albert scratched his head. ''Thought I heard someone yelling over this way.''

"Uh, Red lost her shoe, that's all."

"Yeah, in the water," she added, nodding vigorously.

Clay pointed at the bottom of the boat to Red's bare foot to prove his point. He looked to the spot where he'd pointed and connected with a bright blue condom packet twinkling in the sunlight.

"Well, dang," said Uncle Albert. "Not everybody can lose a shoe in a little rowboat like this in the middle of a flood. Takes a lot of determination." Uncle Albert glanced from Clay to Red, who looked as if she'd been out in the sun too long, and said, "You know, one shoe's not much good. Wouldn't hurt much if you went and lost the other one, too."

Uncle Albert revved the outboard and slowly turned his boat back toward shore. Red gripped Clay's hand. "What are we going to do?"

He grinned. "We could work on losing that other shoe."

"Clay!"

"Uncle Albert won't say a word. He's not a gossip. But we do have to get back and see when the fresh water trucks will get here and what conditions the roads are in."

He checked his watch. "I'm sure it won't be long before help gets to us. We need food and medical supplies. Hell, we need everything. We should be seeing some relief by late afternoon."

A half hour later as Clay sat on a pile of old tires

in Sam's welding shed watching the news of the flood on his generator-powered TV, Clay realized he'd been right about Uncle Albert, but totally wrong about when help would arrive. He'd missed that one by a mile.

Jake and Sam leaned against the workbench and Red sat on an unopened case of motor oil. All of them speechless, staring at the screen, not wanting to believe it would be two days before help got to the more remote areas of the Eastern Shore. And that meant Paradise Creek.

Jake paced the cramped area. "Who would have thought a hurricane that never reached land would cause so darn much trouble? Looks like it dumped tons of rain everywhere east of the Bay."

Clay shook his head. "And help's going to the bigger towns first."

He tried to rid himself of the feeling of desperation settling in around him. Damn, he wanted to pace. He really needed to, but there was only room for one pacer at a time. "How are *we* supposed to live without water? Just because we're a small town, we're last on the 'help' list? When it comes to paying our taxes we sure as hell aren't last. I don't hear anyone saying, 'Oh, you're just a little town on the Eastern Shore where there aren't many people, so you all can pay your taxes on April seventeenth or eighteenth or whenever you get around to it.'"

A crooked smile slid across Sam's face. "Guess

we're on our own for a spell. We need to make some plans. I got the two backhoes; one's not running so good, but we can start clearing the streets of debris as the water drops. We'll just keep our fingers crossed the equipment doesn't break down, and repair it fast if it does.''

Jake said, ''I'll get the volunteer fire department together. They can hose down some of the mud before it dries. We need to determine drop-off points where all things ruined by the flood can be discarded. And we should make a priority list of what's to be cleaned off first.''

Clay rubbed the back of his neck. ''This is just terrific. We have to choose what to save. Should it be people's homes, their businesses, churches, roads, the courthouse? How can we make decisions like that?''

He caught sight of Red out of the corner of his eye. She didn't look nearly as cheery as before. She looked as if she'd taken his suggestion on gnashing her teeth. He'd never seen Red look so down.

He turned back to the TV and watched the relief reports. Boats, trucks, supplies were going everywhere, except Paradise Creek. ''Jake, go round up brooms and shovels. Some people have high-pressure washers, and generators can power them. We can stretch out garden hoses. We'll clean up what we can as quick as we can. The water may not be fit for drinking, but it'll work for that.''

Jake nodded. ''I'll have everyone wear boots and

gloves because sanitation's bound to be a problem. We should have electricity restored to some of the houses by noon.''

Clay looked at Red. She was sitting there, gazing into space, fiddling with the piece of flag they got from Katie's door. ''You okay?''

She didn't look at him, but seemed to be lost in thought. ''There's something I should be doing. I just don't know what it is. My father would know.''

''They can use help at the gym getting food sorted out. You should grab a nap. When the water drops there'll be plenty to do.''

She looked him in the eyes. ''There's something else, Clay, something more.''

He kissed her soundly. ''Get something to eat. You'll feel better.''

He watched Jake and Sam and Red shuffle out of the shed. He kept his eyes on Red till she turned the corner, then he turned back to the TV. As rotten as things were in Paradise Creek—and right now they were plenty rotten and not likely to get better for some time—there was one really good thing in his life. Red.

When he was with her he was totally alive, not just a sheriff doing his duty and taking care of a town. She made him feel things. It might be irritation, or frustration, complete exasperation, but mostly she made him feel happy every time he looked at her, like now, just looking at her on TV.

Huh?

He rubbed his tired eyes and peered at the screen in front of him. Red *was* on TV. This very minute. At least it was a picture of her. Except it wasn't someone named Red-from-D.C., but Hope Stevens, Senator Ashford Stevens's daughter, who was missing. And everyone should be looking their eyeballs-out for her because there was a huge reward for information on her whereabouts. The whole story would be on some show at noon.

Clay felt rooted to where he sat. Red, *his Red,* was Hope Stevens, a *senator's* daughter? Of course she was a senator's daughter. Considering how everything else was going in his life right now, what did he expect? He couldn't just fall for any rich woman from D.C. Hell, no. He had to do it up big. A senator's daughter. A woman surrounded by ultimate power, influence, excitement and flash all her life. Oh yeah, he could really compete with all that as a backwater sheriff living in a clapboard house with his one suit for funerals and weddings.

Elizabeth's family owned a string of department stores and she'd lasted with him and Paradise Creek for less than a year. It was a blooming miracle Red lasted here—and with him—as long as she did.

Well, she wouldn't have to last much longer because he was duty-bound to report missing persons or he'd be obstructing justice. At noon anyone in town with power would see the senator's daughter story on

TV and know about Red. They could turn her in, too. The reward money could help a lot people right now.

He had no choice but to hightail it down to the marina, get on a VHF radio and tell Senator Ashford Stevens his daughter was just fine. He started for the shed door and his gaze fell on the piece of flag lying where she'd sat. He stopped dead.

Dammitall. As angry as he was, and he was spitting angry, he owed her for being with him through this whole mess. And he cared for her one hell of a lot. More than he ever thought possible. Sheriff or not, he couldn't turn her in. Not after what she'd done for Paradise Creek—and for him.

But how could he keep anyone else in town from making that call to the senator? He'd find a way. Somehow. Then he'd ring her little neck for not leveling with him in the first place.

Chapter Eight

Hope couldn't imagine why in the world Clay would call a town meeting in the gym at noon. He insisted everyone be there or answer to him. With so much going on, why meet now? Getting everyone together at that time seemed of primary importance. *But why?* Mrs. Rowley might know what was going on. Being plugged in to the Paradise Creek gossip system had definite advantages.

But where was Mrs. Rowley? Hope hadn't seen her since last night, when they'd walked down Main Street together, arm in arm. Hope's throat tightened, her eyes stung with tears. She'd never forget that night as long as she lived, and she'd never forget the people of Paradise Creek.

Hope spied Mrs. Rowley on the bleachers and headed in that direction. Everyone in the gym looked as if they needed a vacation, except Mrs. Rowley. She looked as if she'd just returned. Bright eyes, rosy face, warm smile. How'd she do that after such a terrible night?

They exchanged greetings as Hope sat down, and asked, "Any damage on The Gray? I haven't had a chance to look at it."

Mrs. Rowley smiled. "Last night I stayed with Al—I mean…ah…my family. Checked on The Gray this morning. Just some mud washed over the porches. Albert's house is the same way. The creeks did the flooding, not the Bay. Nice that The Gray is on the Bay side. But some of the others…" She pursed her lips and shook her head, looking incredibly sad. "They didn't fare nearly so well. A few of the houses have electricity now. That means the town's on the mend." She patted Hope's hand. "I wonder how Clay's holding up."

As if on cue, he walked on to the stage. He looked around as if mentally taking role call, making sure everyone was there. He paced, checked his watch, then talked about extra food stored at the gym, getting generators from the boats at the marina and how everyone needed to wear gloves when cleaning up.

Mrs. Rowley whispered, "Everybody knows this. Clay keeps looking at his watch like something's going to happen."

He suddenly quit talking midsentence and told everyone to go.

For a moment a stunned silence hung in the air that clearly suggested Sheriff Clay Mitchell was completely off his rocker. As everyone filed out of the gym, they exchanged quizzical looks and gave Clay a wide berth in case whatever he had was contagious.

Mrs. Rowley said, "We need to check on that boy. Not behaving like his usual know-it-all self. Wonder what's wrong with him."

She looked at Hope. "Heard you and Clay lost a shoe or two while in that rowboat this morning. Anything go wrong since then?"

"Does everyone in town know about…my shoes?"

"Honey, it's a little town and we're all desperate for gossip that doesn't have the words rain or flood in it. When Albert came back from looking for you and Clay, smiling like a baboon with a crate of bananas, we grilled the poor man till he cracked." She winked. "He didn't have a chance."

As they got to Clay, Sam burst through the double gym doors. "The backhoe died," he said as he came over to Clay. "We're down to one. Now what?"

Jake and Albert came in the side door. Albert said, "We've got enough fresh water to last the town through the night, and then I don't know what we're going to do."

Clay rubbed the back of his neck. "Tell Ruth Owens to set up a ration program. She's good at organizing that way, and, Sam, get your guys on that backhoe."

His eyes went deep-set and his lips thinned. Her heart ached for him because this was his town. Everyone depended on Clay to make things right, and there was so little he could do. If she could help him in any way she'd do it in a heartbeat.

Jake said, "Well, Red. You left one mess in D.C., and landed yourself smack in the middle of ours. Compared to the problems of Paradise Creek, I'm guessing D.C. is looking pretty good to you right now."

"*Ohmygosh!* That's it! D.C." She kissed Jake. "And you're right, it is looking good. Wonderful, in fact. My father. All I have to do is call him. Everything will be fine, or at least closer to fine than it is now."

CLAY STARED AT Red's retreating figure in total disbelief. He didn't have to worry about his decision *not* to call Senator Ashford Stevens to come get his daughter. And he didn't have to arrange this meeting to keep anyone else from calling. And he didn't have to wonder how long it would take Red to tire of Paradise Creek and him. She already had, and she was leaving. "She didn't even say goodbye."

Jake rubbed his stubbled chin. "She's only going to make a phone call, Clay."

Clay shoved his hands into his pockets. "She's leaving. As soon as Jake suggested D.C. she was happy as a kid at Christmas, and took off like a bullet. Can you think of anything else that would make her happy, except getting out of here and going back to D.C.? Hell, why would she want to stay?''

Uncle Albert tipped his fishing hat to the back of his head. ''I don't know where you're getting this, boy, or why she'd call home. Fact is, I always thought it was the last thing on Red's mind. But no matter, Red's not the kind to up and leave just because we're having problems. Seems to me the girl thrives on problems, attracts them like bees to honey. Hell, she's attracted to you, isn't she?''

Clay let out a deep sigh. ''You all don't know it, but Red's a senator's daughter—Hope Stevens, Senator Ashford Steven's daughter. And D.C. and her father have got to be looking one hell of a lot better to her than a flooded town with no electricity and a sheriff who can't even save his...''

He stopped talking and looked from Mrs. Rowley to Uncle Albert to Jake. ''Why don't any of you look surprised that Red is a senator's daughter?''

Uncle Albert's eyes widened. ''Oh, we're surprised, Clay.'' He looked at Mrs. Rowley. ''Aren't we, Lettie? Shocked to our socks, yessirree bob. That's us.''

''Bunk! You all knew who she was all the time.''

''Us?'' Jake shrugged.

''I don't believe this. You all knew and none of you told me?''

Uncle Albert took off his hat and ran his fingers through his hair. ''Whole town knows, and we didn't tell you because we know you take your duties as sheriff real serious and would hand her over because she was a missing person. But, Red—rather, Hope—belongs here. Saved Willow Pond Church and Bobby, helped Jake win over Carlie Lewis, got me and Lettie together. No one in Paradise Creek would turn her in. She's part of this town and she's not going anywhere."

Clay growled, "You should have turned her in and got the reward money because she's gone now."

Mrs. Rowley tipped her chin and lowered her gaze. "Why didn't *you* turn her in if you knew who she was?"

Clay shoved open the double doors of the gym with Mrs. Rowley's words ringing in his ears and feeding his guilt. He might be angry with Red for leaving, but he was furious with himself for falling for her in the first place, and for putting her before his duty as sheriff. Fact is, he didn't deserve to be sheriff after a stunt like that. What was wrong with him? He'd put her before the very thing he loved most—his job.

Didn't his marriage to Elizabeth teach him anything? *Rich girls don't fall for poor boys, Clay Mitchell.* That's what she'd told him when the divorce was final, as if it explained away everything. Too bad he didn't take it to heart.

HOPE HELPED Ruth Owens and Mabel Farley sweep the sidewalks, while Mrs. Rowley and Carlie Lewis used garden hoses to squirt down everything after most of the mud was removed.

A cruiser rounded the corner and Clay pulled to the curb. He got out and came her way. He looked more tired and worried than ever with deep circles under his bloodshot eyes.

"When's your rescue party going to arrive?"

"How…did you know a rescue party was on its way? I can't believe this. I just made the call to D.C. a few minutes ago. Paradise Creek gossips are incredible."

"Don't need gossips to figure out the obvious. You said you were going to call home."

She beamed. "I called my father."

"No kidding."

She paused and studied him. "Why are you so upset? My father can help straighten things out. He's a senator and has a lot of authority."

Jake came over and patted her on the back and said to Clay, "Did Red tell you the news?"

Mrs. Rowley came across the street. "Heard you gave that senator father of yours a call. My stars, what did the man say when you asked for help?"

Hope shrugged. "'Done.' Then he hung up."

Mrs. Rowley huffed, "What's that supposed to mean? Don't think I ever heard a politician use so few words. Usually it's blah, blah, blah…"

Albert came around the corner, looking like a conquering hero. "Glad I found you all." He turned to

Clay. "Guess what, boy. I hooked a couple generators up at the gym. We've got hot cocoa and coffee brewing and Katie's whipping up soup. Am I a genius or what?"

He put his arm around Mrs. Rowley and continued, "'Course fresh water would be nice." He grinned at Hope. "Heard from Jake that you contacted your father." Then he smiled at Mrs. Rowley. "I think I deserve a kiss for all my hard work, don't you?"

Mrs. Rowley blushed, and her lips met Albert's in a kiss that was obviously not their first. Hope glanced at Clay and flashed him a smile that said, *isn't this romance great?* But he ignored her completely. In fact, he looked right through her as if she didn't exist.

Now what the heck was that all about? When she glanced and smiled, she expected a glance and a smile in return, especially from the man she'd seduced in a rowboat this morning, and who was half the reason she just called her father.

The Jones brothers pulled up in their trucks, complete with shoveling blades on the front. "Guess you're all talking about Red calling her dad. Word's all over town."

Billy Jones gave her a friendly wink, Clay fired off a look that could kill and Sam came up the street waving a piece of paper. "Hey, Red, one of the guys from the marina just ran this up to me. Said I should give it to you. Your dad's sending a boat. Should be here by three at the latest."

Hope said, "A boat? Better be a big one."

Clay groused, "You're not content with getting the hell out of here, you want it on some damn aircraft carrier. Maybe you want a helicopter or a fighter jet escort, too?"

Billy shook his head. "What in the world are you talking about, Clay? Why are you being so damn disagreeable? What's up?"

Clay's face pulled into hard lines, his sheriff's face firmly in place. He said to Billy, "You stay the hell out of this." He turned to Hope. "Nothing's up with me. If you want to run away every time things get tough, that's your business. Paradise Creek will get along without you just fine. We did it before, we can do it again. Don't bother to write."

Everyone was quiet and Uncle Albert shook his head "You're digging yourself into a mighty deep hole."

Hope said, "I thought you knew what was going on. My father—"

"Is coming to rescue his darling daughter and take her back to the lap of luxury." Clay turned for his cruiser. "If you want to give her a going-away party because of all she's done around here, go for it, but don't invite me. I'm not interested."

Billy said, "Clay, you're getting yourself into some deep doo-doo here."

Hope stared at Clay, letting his words sink in. She

pulled in a deep breath. "Why would you think I'm leaving?"

"Why would you stay?"

She planted her hands on her hips. "Because I like Paradise Creek. Because this town is the best thing that's ever happened to me, even though it happens to have a first-class tyrannical nincompoop and close-minded bureaucrat for a sheriff. You're so sure you've got all the answers, you're not listening to me or anyone else. Well, listen to this, big shot. I called my father on one of those boat radios down at the marina. They beamed me up to my father's office and, since he is a senator with considerable influence and is a man of his word, Paradise Creek should have water and power and anything else it needs by late afternoon."

Jake cleared his throat. "It's 'VHF' and 'patched you through.'"

"Right. And that boat that's coming isn't to snare me away to the lap of riches, but to bring water and supplies and hoses and whatever to the town."

Clay turned slowly. He didn't seem to be breathing.

Mrs. Farley said, "Better be cooking up crow for dinner, Clay's going to be eating a plateful. Having humble pie for dessert."

Jake added, "Somebody fetch Doc over here. Clay's got his foot stuck in his mouth, big-time."

"I'm finished with you. Your arrogance makes my

father and ex-fiancé look like shrinking violets in that department.''

''But I thought—''

''I didn't hear you ask, 'Hey, Red, are you going back to D.C., or are you sticking around for a while to help us out here?'''

She kicked the cruiser tire. ''Somewhere along the line, you got the idea I'm a snob, that I can only live in D.C., and could never be happy here because nothing in Paradise Creek could ever interest me.'' She looked him straight in the eyes. ''That *you* could never interest me.'' She got to within an inch of his face. ''Now hear this—you interest me, Clay Mitchell, but you also make me mad as hell. I'd be a damn fool to ever get involved with you and your overbearing attitude.''

She reached into her pocket and pulled out the star he'd given her. She tossed it on top of the hood of the cruiser and it skidded across and sailed off the other side. ''Find yourself another deputy. I quit.''

She turned for the marina and heard Clay say, ''Hope, wait. Please.''

But she didn't. She was too darn mad at the moment. She stomped her way down to the marina to watch for the promised boat. Her shoes crunched on the stones and anger ate at her. Clay hadn't changed one iota from the day she met him. He was no different now than when she smashed into that tree and he ordered her to get out of that van. He was Napoleon, only bigger.

"Hey, Red." It was Jake. "Wait up." He jogged up and fell in step beside her. "Mind if I walk with you for a minute? Look, I realize Clay was as dumb as a box of rocks just now, but I want you to know, in spite of everything, he's really a great guy."

"You got the 'box of rocks' part right."

"He's just had a rough life. A lot of people have run out on him—his mom, Elizabeth. He thought you were doing the same."

Hope stopped in the middle of the gravel road. "He could have asked, you know. He didn't have to assume that I had the sense of little green apples and the loyalty of a slug."

"But you two are great together. You—"

Hope glared at Jake, cutting him off.

He took a few steps back. "Or not. Think I'll go shovel some dirt. Think I'll go mind my own beeswax."

"Good idea." Hope watched Jake walk back up the roadway. He turned and yelled, "I really do think you two are good together. You and Clay got everybody in town to safety, remember that? Great teamwork."

"You can't sweet-talk me, Jake. I know the game—my father's a politician." Though she did feel good about helping Clay get everyone out of town. At times, she and Clay *were* good together, but too often the qualities that made him an excellent sheriff did not make him an excellent partner in a relationship. Maybe because the word "partner" was a foreign concept to him.

Mrs. Rowley passed Jake as she came down the road and hooked her arm through Hope's. She tugged her to a bench. "Mind if we talk a spell? Good. Now I know you're cross as nine highways with our resident sheriff, but Clay is the way he is because he feels responsible for this town. Almost losing it has made him overreact a bit."

"A bit?"

"I think if you gave him another chance you'd see he's a lot more bark than bite."

"I don't want any part of Clay's barking or his overreacting. He can do whatever he darn well wants as long as it doesn't involve me."

"But you two could be happy together."

"He's bossy and that's not going to change."

"He's handsome."

"You got me there." Hope gave Mrs. Rowley a hard look out of the corner of her eye.

"Guess I should be going. I imagine Katie could use a little help making dinner. Try and concentrate on the handsome part, dear." She winked at Hope. "You're just what he needs 'cause you'll stand up to him, and I suspect he's what you need, too. I doubt if you respect anyone like you respect Clay Mitchell."

Hope watched Mrs. Rowley make her way up the road and exchange a few words with Albert as he came down. It was a parade! Hope swallowed a groan as Albert gave her a weak smile and took her hand.

"I know Clay's got you in a stew right now, missy, and sometimes he just doesn't know when to keep his mouth shut—"

"I am not getting together with Clay because the whole town thinks I should."

"He did what he did because he was afraid he'd lost you."

"He didn't even ask me if I was lost or not. He just assumed the worst."

"Hum. Maybe I should go check on those generators."

Hope didn't bother to watch Albert leave. She didn't want to see who else was beating a path to her to extol the virtues of Sheriff Clay Mitchell. But there was little doubt that everyone in Paradise Creek loved Clay.

"Red?" It was Clay, the last person on earth she wanted to talk to.

She pushed herself from the bench and faced him. Eyes deep-set, chin needing a shave, a smear of dirt across his forehead, responsibility resting squarely on his broad shoulders. For a second she wanted to wrap her arms around him, offer support. Then the second passed and she remembered she'd rather offer the creep a kick in the shins. "If you're here to tell me you acted like a jackass today because you had a tough childhood, or because you're tired, or because Elizabeth left you, or some other cockamamie excuse, save your breath. I've already heard it and a lot more from everyone else around here who still think you walk on water and make the sun come up each morning."

"I came to thank you for calling your father."

"Oh." Well that took the wind right out of her sails. "I did it for the town. Paradise Creek." She gave him a defiant look.

His lips thinned. "You could have told me you were calling him to ask for help."

"In case you forgot, I just ran out on a wedding he'd planned and a future son-in-law he endorsed for the senate. I wasn't sure if I'd get the prodigal daughter treatment, or be kicked out of the family home on my derriere. No need to get everyone's hopes up for nothing."

"A hint would have been nice."

"Trust would have been nice. Everyone else here has faith in me. Mrs. Rowley, Jake, Ruth Owens and the rest never made demands or asked questions. They accepted me and knew I'd be there for them, unlike some big guy in a tan uniform who shall remain nameless." She poked him in the chest with her index finger. "I bet not a single one of those other people thought I was running back to D.C."

"They also didn't have to find out who the hell

you were from a TV ad over at Sam's shed. It wasn't exactly thrown in their faces. You trusted them and told them who you were."

"You would have turned me in."

He looked her dead in the eyes. "I didn't turn you in when I had the chance."

"Why not?"

He raked his hair with his left and let out a deep sigh. "Maybe because you put your life on the line for this town and...I owed you." He shook his head. "I should have...and why I didn't beats the living hell out of me."

"It's because you don't have any faith in me."

He shook his head. "It's not that I don't have faith in you, it's that I don't..."

"Don't what?"

He glanced up the gravel road and heaved a deep sigh. "Are you still mad?"

"Heck, yes."

"Well, you better get over it. Your father's here."

"*What?*"

"Red hair, bad temper, designer clothes. Basic family characteristics."

Her eyes popped. Her jaw dropped—probably to her toes—before she could stop it. A queasy feeling rumbled through her stomach. She cracked her knuckles. "He's on the marine radio. Right? That's what you mean by here."

"Try Paradise Creek. Can't see hair and clothes on

a radio. A man on a mission. You've got a hell of gene pool going there, Red.''

She peered at the water and the docks. "*Why did he come?* He has work to do. He *always* has work to do." She waved her hand at the marina. "Where's the boat? The supplies? And I take after my mother's side, a very gentle woman, and *I do not have a temper.*"

"Apparently the senator contacted a contingent of The National Guard already in the county and had them come straight to us. They all came by truck, clearing the roads on the way. Water jugs are being dispersed. Electricity crews are already at work and everything's getting hosed.''

Clay's look turned sincere. His eyes the bluest ever, and he came over to her. Her blood went from boiling to slow simmer. "I owe you for this, Red. The whole town does. Calling your dad was the last thing you wanted to do and you put Paradise Creek first. No matter what you think of me, know I appreciate what you did. The Guard can accomplish in hours what it would have taken us days or even weeks to do.''

"For sure he's here? Putting you and him in the same town? Mother have mercy." She swiped her hand over her face. "I should have stayed with the snakes and bugs.''

"Jake and the rest can keep him running around in circles for only so long. I wanted to give you fair warning of what was—''

"Hope?"

She didn't have to look in the direction of the voice to confirm her suspicions, the hairs standing straight up on the back of her neck were confirmation that her father was indeed here. Suddenly she was aware that her clothes were mussed and her hair undoubtedly looked like a bird's nest.

"Hope? Is that you?"

She took a step away from Clay and watched Senator Ashford Stevens stride briskly down the gravel drive. Then again, Senator Stevens always strode briskly. He did everything briskly. Sunlight glistened off his perfectly styled auburn-splashed-with-silver hair that no wind from a helicopter or any other wind would dare to ruffle. As usual, his understated tie hung loosely but fashionably at his neck and the sleeves of his blue button-down shirt were neatly rolled back working-man's style. She'd picked out that very outfit for him.

"Dad? I...I didn't expect you to come here."

He drew up in front of her, looking as if he were posing for a photo shoot. It was a gift, one she didn't inherit. He was always the perfect image of a U.S. senator. "You've been gone for almost two weeks without any word and you didn't think I'd come running once I found you? Can't believe that even a little town like this didn't get a fax or see the tabloids or something about you being missing and get a hold of me before this. The media had a field day. Who's in charge around here?''

Clay held out his hand. "That would be me.''

Hope said, "This is Sheriff Clay Mitchell.''

The two men shook hands and sized each other up, as men always do. Women admire each other's shoes and do lunch.

Her father gave Clay a pointed look and continued, "You didn't get any word of Hope being missing?''

"Dad, we've got other things to think about right now. It's been hectic around here.''

"The Guard's in charge now. You can get your things together. We're going home. I don't have a lot of time—''

"Then *you* go on back to D.C.'' The words came out in one quick breath. Hope swallowed a gasp. She couldn't believe she'd said that and, from the look on her father's face, he couldn't believe it, either. She clenched her fists and pushed on, hoping the rest would come to her through some divine intervention. "I'm needed here, and you certainly don't need me in D.C.''

A deep vee furrowed between her father's eyebrows. "Kenneth is frantic with worry.''

Hope felt as if lightning zapped her. For this confrontation she didn't need any intervention at all. "I don't see Kenneth anywhere around here, do you?'' She waved her hand across the Bay. "My guess is the little weasel is doing damage control over the wedding, working on the female sympathy vote and has his beady little eye on another well-connected bride.''

She knew her father well enough to catch that little glint in his eye when someone made a point he wished hadn't been made at all. That glint was there right now, looking more like a neon light.

He said, ''You can't go wandering around the countryside. You'll look irresponsible. I'll look bad as your father. No good will come of it.''

''I'm twenty-nine. It's time I do a little wandering. And I promise not to rob banks or knock over little old ladies along the way.'' She sent Clay a look that said, *mention one word about the wrecked van and you're dead meat.*

She continued, ''I've got things to do here, people I want to help because they helped me. I'll call Kenneth as soon as the phones are working. You and he can tell the press whatever you want. I don't really care.''

''You ran out on your wedding, Hope. Don't you think you owe him more than a phone call?''

She stiffened her spine and stood tall. ''At least I didn't plan on running for the senate on my wife's name. I think he owes me an apology, though I suspect hell will freeze over before it happens.''

Her father's lips drew into a thin line and his gray eyes turned steely. ''You'll come home now.''

Clay interrupted, "With all due respect, Senator, Red wants to stay and that should be her right—"

"Red? Who's Red? My daughter's name is Hope, and who the hell are you to tell me what to do? You might be sheriff around here, but that doesn't give you the right to come between me and my daughter. Find something else to butt into besides my affairs."

Clay's eyes hinted of glacial ice. He stood toe-to-toe with Senator Ashford Stevens. Hope had never seen anyone have the guts to do that on Capitol Hill or anywhere else. Clay said, "If Red wants to stay in Paradise Creek, then that's where she's going to stay. Got it?"

Her father's nose was an inch from Clay's. There was a firm set to his chin. "She's my daughter. She's coming back to D.C. with me where she belongs. *You got that?*"

"She's staying in Paradise Creek. She belongs here. She's a part of this town. Ask anyone."

"I don't have to ask about my own daughter and her town is across the Bay. She's coming with me."

"I don't think so."

Hope waved her hands in the air. "That's it! Stop! I don't believe this." She shook her head. "Actually I do believe it and that's the trouble. You're both talking about me like I'm not even here. Listen to yourselves trying to rule my life. I don't know which of you is worse. And I'm fed up to my eyeballs with both of you."

Chapter Nine

She faced her father. "I'm staying in Paradise Creek. There's nothing for me in D.C. I'm making my home here."

The little blue vein in her father's temple beat double-time. "And how will you live? Answer me that. Sell pencils on the street corners?"

She put her hands to her hips. "Since I left D.C. I've survived a flood, bugs, the threat of snakes, painted an entire office, been trapped on a roof and kept the king of Paradise Creek over there from finding out who I am. If I can do all those things, getting a job will undoubtedly be a *piece of cake.*"

He looked stunned. Had she ever seen him stunned before? Had anyone?

She turned to Clay. "And you can get that *I won* smirk off your face. Just because I'm staying in Paradise Creek has nothing to do with you. You're still bossy and arrogant, worse than ever, and as you can see—" she nodded at her father "—I've had my fill.

You'll both be bellowing orders till the day you die, trying to tell me and everyone else in the world what to do and how to do it. But that doesn't mean I have to be around either of you to listen to it." She looked from one to the other. "I'm finished with both of you."

She turned on her heel and stomped up the gravel road. She could feel her father's and Clay's gazes following her, but there was not one word from either of them. For once, the two most domineering men in all of North America were completely speechless.

DUSK DARKENED to night as Clay plopped himself down on the front steps of the courthouse with a six-pack of lukewarm beer for company. He gazed down Main Street. Sometimes a six-pack at any temperature made for damn good company, and this was definitely one of those times. He was tired. Tired from the flood, the cleanup and, most of all, he was tired from the two confrontations he'd had with Red, both of which he managed to lose royally.

The buildings on Main Street were still dark since electricity hadn't been restored to this section yet. But even though he couldn't see details, he knew the cleanup was well under way. Heavy mud had been shoveled out of the homes and businesses; ruined furnishings had been carted off to the dump. The Eastern Shore had been declared a disaster area and low-interest loans would be available. It was a start at getting things back to the way they were. A big start. Last night he wasn't sure he'd ever be able to say that.

He heard footsteps, men's, leather on pavement. Not a common sound in these parts unless someone was getting married. He knew it was Senator Stevens before he paused and said, "Spare a desperate man a beer?"

Clay looked up and realized it wasn't Senator Ashford Stevens on the sidewalk but a man miserable over losing his only daughter. Clay nodded at the space beside him. He twisted two cans from plastic rings and handed one over to Stevens as he sat down. Clay snapped open the can. The senator did the same, then tapped his can against Clay's. "To Paradise Creek."

"To Paradise Creek," Clay agreed and savored a long drink. "Senator, I want to thank you for your help."

Stevens swiped his lips with the back of his hand in an un-senator-like gesture. "Floods are hell. You're lucky you didn't lose anyone."

"Got your daughter to thank for that. She sort of propelled people into action."

The senator took another drink and gazed off into the darkness. "She sure isn't the girl that left D.C. nine days ago. Don't know what's come over her. She's different. Different as mustard and custard. Used to be all sweet and easygoing. Now she's all spit and vinegar. Not that I'm complaining, mind you. Just surprised all to hell and back.''

Clay felt as if he'd been slapped upside the head with a dictionary. "I have to tell you, that's not the reaction I expected. And right now you don't sound anything like you did this afternoon at the docks." He took a long swig of beer. "You sound…country."

"Hell, man, I'm a senator. It pained me deeply to think my daughter was a wuss, but I don't much understand how she got the way she is now. And as far as sounding country, that's 'cause I'm bilingual." He gave Clay a crooked smile. "Born and raised in Sweet Water, West Virginia, not too different than Paradise Creek. Got an Ivy League education on a scholarship, married a gal from Boston and went into politics. Acquired my second language along the way." He smiled. "But sometimes, when I'm real tired and kind of down like I am now, I'm back in Sweet Water."

Clay raised his can. "To Sweet Water."

Both men tossed back their brews and Clay peeled off two more cans and said, "It was the wedding that turned your daughter around, you know. When she showed up here she was mad as a bear with a sore paw about you marrying her off to some political upstart. Refused to go back to D.C. and wouldn't even give me her name."

Stevens pulled the tab and Clay greeted Ruth Owens as she strolled up the street with an armload of blankets. Stevens said, "Funny about that wedding. I thought I was doing the right thing and now it looks like I might have lost Hope forever. I wanted her to marry Kenneth because I thought she needed someone to take care of her. She didn't seem to have any direction, though she's damn good at selecting my wardrobe, I'll give her that. Made D.C.'s best-dressed list eight years in a row now. Anyway, I figured since I was in politics and Kenneth wanted to go into politics, it was something she knew. A few minutes before the wedding I got cold feet, so I put that campaign button in her bouquet. She needed to know what was going on, what kind of man she was marrying."

Clay stopped mid-drink. "*You* put that campaign button in her bouquet? She put a lot of stock in finding that button and she needs to know you put it there. It'll make a difference, I guarantee it."

Stevens rotated his beer between his palms and studied it as if it held some secret. "I tried to marry her off like some tyrannical father from the Middle Ages. The woman I saw at the docks is not going to get over that too easily."

"You're her father. All she wants from you is your love and to know that you care. *You,* she'll forgive. *Me,* she'll torment."

Clay handed a third beer to Stevens as he said, "My daughter's sure got her knickers in a knot over something going on between you two."

"She thinks I'm bossy."

The senator raised an eyebrow that asked *that's it?*

"And arrogant. And that I don't have any faith in her and that I won't change. This afternoon when I stood up to you at the docks I thought I was helping by taking her side." He shrugged and took a drink. "In Red's book, bossy is bossy. I'm the sheriff. I tell people what to do."

"With or without a uniform?"

Clay nodded and finished off the third beer. Stevens did the same, then said, "You're the kind of man who goes after what he wants. If you had it in your head you wanted Hope, you'd be turning this town upside down to have her. What's holding you back, Sheriff? When it comes to women it's usually one of two things—some woman did you wrong and you don't want to go through that again. Or you don't know if you have what it takes to keep her happy."

Clay studied the sidewalk in front of him. "Try both."

Stevens gave him a crooked smile. "If you want her, you're going to have to take a chance just like the rest of us do sooner or later."

Stevens let out a deep breath. "Least you'll be here with her to work it out. I have meetings tomorrow on a pending bill that can't be put off. A car's coming to take me back to D.C. at ten."

Clay glanced at his watch. "It's nine. There's time for you to talk to Hope. She's probably at The Gray.

It's on Bay Street, you can't miss it. Think of this as a campaign speech to get reelected as Hope's father.''

"Think I'll campaign as Hope's dad this time." He flashed an encouraged grin as he stood. "And it's going to be the most important reelection of my life."

HOPE SAT DOWN on the porch swing and gazed across the Bay. Thank heavens she was on this side of water and not the other. Paradise Creek might be an hour's drive from D.C., but it was light-years away in many other ways. She gave a little kick and set the swing into a gentle rock. Staying in Paradise Creek was the best decision she ever made, next to running away from that blasted wedding and vowing to stay away from his lordship, Sheriff Clay Mitchell.

Trouble was, she was having a devil of a time convincing her hormones that avoiding Clay was a great idea. At this very minute they were waging war to convince her otherwise. She felt hot, then cold, then…steamy, very steamy, whenever she thought about Clay, which was continuously. She fanned herself with her hand.

"Hope?"

"Dad?" She jumped, nearly toppling the swing over backwards.

"You were in deep thought over something." He looked down at her, in the moonlight his eyes were a soft gray and not hard and insisting as usual. "Room for one more on that swing?"

She looked around as if some other person suddenly appeared on the porch. "*You* want to... swing?"

He sat down and she joined him as he said, "This is a great swing. Oak. The best kind. Nice house."

"You smell like a brewery."

"A small brewery. I came to tell you that I'm sorry about the mess with Kenneth. I really thought he was good for you."

"S-sorry?" Her father knew this word? Could use it in a sentence? "In some ways Kenneth was good for me. He made me realize what I *didn't* want in life and that I had to change if I ever intended to make a life of my own." She smiled and shrugged. "But the campaign button you put in my bouquet was the real clincher." She kissed him on the cheek. "Thanks. Thanks for doing it and thanks for coming to tell me you're sorry. Seems like I've been saying thanks to you a lot today." Her smile grew. "I like it."

She watched her father open and shut his mouth a few times, looking like a landed fish, not very Senator Ashford Stevens–like at all. "You knew about the button?"

"As of about two minutes ago. Mrs. Farley didn't have time for any details, but she heard from Mrs. Owens."

Her father wagged his head. "I don't get—"

"The CIA needs to come here, Dad. The communication system is incredible."

Her father kicked the swing into action and pulled in a deep breath. "Guess you're still not coming home?"

"You're...asking? Not telling?"

He let out a long breath and stroked his chin. "I'm trying to be better about that. Your running away scared the hell out of me. I understand why you ran. I knew it was a possibility but I needed to take that chance for your sake and for my own. Couldn't live with myself if I got you into a rotten marriage. I thought you needed someone to take care of you. I was wrong."

He gazed over the Bay. "Paradise Creek is a fine town." He took off his tie and stuffed it in his shirt pocket.

"I don't think I've ever seen you like this."

He grinned. A real grin from the heart that lit up his face and eyes. Not one of those TV or press grins. He said, "I think it's being here. Paradise Creek seems to bring out the best in everybody." He winked at her. "A summer cottage here would be a fine thing. With one of these oak swings." He smacked his arm, then brushed off a squashed mosquito. "Screened-in-porch. Flagpole. Always been partial to flying the Stars and Stripes."

"And a barbecue pit?"

"Good idea."

Hope jumped up. "Okay, that's it. What's going on? What did you have to drink? The Jones brothers' home brew, I bet. I hear it makes you see stars and lots of stripes and everything else. You're drunk as a skunk.''

He motioned for her to sit back down, then said, ''Actually it was your sheriff's brew. We split a six-pack.''

''You drank…beer? Domestic? From a can? With Clay? And you didn't kill each other? What's come over you?''

He gave her a meaningful look and a soft, tender smile. ''I thought I'd lost you, and Clay convinced me I hadn't. I may not have been the most attentive, doting father, Hope, but I've always cared. I want you to know that.''

A lump the size of a basketball lodged in her throat. ''I…know you cared. That's why I went along with what you wanted for so long.''

A black official-looking car crept down the road. Stones crushed under the tires as it rolled to a stop and the headlights dimmed.

''Your ride?''

''I'll be back soon to pick out a house. That you can bet on.'' He shrugged. ''I don't want to miss anything.'' He stood and gently stroked her cheek.

''It's Paradise Creek, Dad. There's not much to miss. That's the beauty of the place.''

He put his hand on her shoulder. ''That's before you showed up and knocked that sheriff right out of his saddle.'' Her father laughed. ''Your mother did the same thing to me over thirty years ago. Shame she didn't live to see the tradition carried on. She would have been tickled pink, Hope.''

He kissed her forehead, then jogged down the steps to the waiting car. She watched the taillights fade in the darkness. Never in a million years did she expect to have this conversation with her father. She thought any real relationship died when she ran out on the wedding.

Her father had changed. Their relationship had taken giant steps forward and that was wonderful. He respected her opinion and understood how she felt. No daughter could ask for more. But he was mistaken about Clay. Getting involved with him would be the end of her new-found independence. He'd run over her like a charging bull.

No bulls, no charging, no losing her independence, and Clay Mitchell would stay in the saddle. Tomorrow, Tuesday, when the whole town would be out cleaning and fixing and she saw Clay, she'd have to make herself remember *that* and not how they'd survived a flood, saved a town and lost a shoe in a rowboat.

HOPE SHIELDED HER EYES from the morning sun as she walked down Main Street toward Katie's Kitchen to help with clearing out the back storage room. The sidewalks teemed with people scraping and scrubbing and sweeping. She felt Clay's presence, then turned around and saw him crossing the street toward her. "Hey, Red, wait up."

He looked better, more rested. She thought of her resolution from last night and steeled herself against his good looks.

"Did your dad get off okay?"

"He's fine. We're fine, thanks to you and the beer."

He raised his eyebrows.

"Okay, we're more than fine." Even though there were many people on the street, Clay's presence overshadowed everyone else. Yep, charging bull.

"Yoo-hoo," Mrs. Rowley called from across the street. She and Albert stood in front of Something's Fishy, sweeping the sidewalk. They both waved like mad, as if they were sailing off on an around-the-world cruise on the *QE II*. They headed across the street, arm in arm.

Clay said, "Uncle Albert wasn't home last night."

"Neither was Mrs. Rowley," Hope mumbled. "I think we should ground them...."

"I think I'm jealous."

"Hello, dears," said Mrs. Rowley. "Isn't it a glorious day?"

She waved her left hand in the air, taking in the whole town, the Bay, everything. Mrs. Rowley was very energetic this morning. And happy. Incredibly so. A repercussion from being out all night?

Mrs. Rowley continued, "And the town's sprucing up so nice."

She waved again with a gracefully outstretched hand. "It's all coming together much quicker than we all expected, thanks to your father and those wonderful soldiers. Where are they now?" She cupped her cheek with her left hand and wiggled her fingers.

"My father left last night and The Guard's— What is that on your left hand?"

Mrs. Rowley fluttered her eyes, smiled hugely and extended her hand like a reigning queen. "That is an engagement ring."

Sunlight set fire to a lovely ruby in an antique setting. She looked from Clay to Albert to Hope, and said, "Albert and I are getting married, and I want you to be my maid of honor. My daughter agrees, since Albert and I would have never gotten together if it wasn't for you giving me a little encouragement and making me feel good about myself again."

Albert patted Mrs. Rowley's arm. "I never knew you'd be interested in an old geezer like me, Lettie. Life can sure be wonderful." He looked at Clay. "And I'd be honored if you'd be my best man."

"I'm so happy for you." Hope kept a smile plastered on her face as the ramifications of all this sunk in. Albert and Mrs. Rowley getting married *was* terrific, but she and Clay in that wedding was the pits! As much as witnessing Mrs. Rowley's wedding was indeed an honor, she suspected it was also a last-ditch effort to get her and Clay together. Seniors could be very crafty that way.

Hope said, "Ever think about eloping? Vegas. Just the two of you. No flood. Everything bright and clean." Hope waved her hand over the town. "Proper clothes and food will be a problem if you get married here. In Vegas that won't be any problem at all." She crossed her fingers and prayed for the wisdom of her words to sink in.

Albert tisked. "Wouldn't dream of getting married any place but Paradise Creek. Here with all our friends and family. We're thinking Sunday's a good day. Don't want to waste any time. The flood made us realize how short life is and how precious. Lettie and I took each other for granted for years." He shook his head. "Not anymore. We treasure each day we have together."

Happiness danced in his eyes. "And we've decided to tie the knot at Willow Pond Church. It will have to be outside the church, of course, but the weather is supposed to hold and it'll be a grand party for all of us. We can celebrate Paradise Creek making it through the flood with everyone safe and Lettie and me beginning a new life together. This town shares in good times and in bad. We figured we all just shared the bad, now it's time for the good."

So much for wisdom. Was kismet bringing her and Clay together? Fate? Destiny? More like a persistent town refusing to give up on the two of them.

Hope kissed Mrs. Rowley on the cheek. "I'd be delighted to be your maid of honor. We can make a trip into D.C. tomorrow and shop for—"

Mrs. Rowley shook her head. "I think we should use what we have here in Paradise Creek. What we've salvaged. It's a promise for the future, take what we have and move on."

Uncle Albert added, "We think if the whole town pitched in it will get their minds off what we lost and concentrate on what was spared."

Hope felt a smile creep over her face. "It's a good idea. I like it."

She glanced at Clay and he nodded in agreement as Albert said, "I'm thrilled to hear you both say that because Lettie and I are leaving the planning in your very capable hands. We just wouldn't know where to begin to organize something like this in our advanced years and all."

Mrs. Rowley added, "It'll be like your wedding present to us. Something we'll never forget."

Clay folded his arms. "Advanced years? You two are playing us like a fiddle at a square dance."

Uncle Albert smiled hugely. "Well, of course we are. People of advanced years are allowed to do such things." He took Mrs. Rowley's arm. "And Hope, you don't have to help Katie in her kitchen. Lettie and I are doing that. You and Clay just put your heads together and concentrate on the wedding, or whatever else comes to mind."

Hope pointed down the street. "I said I'd help Katie and I really should."

Mrs. Rowley shrugged. "If that's really the way you feel, dear, then by all means you should go, but I heard they pulled out three snakes at that end of town. Guess they took up living there to eat up all the water bugs."

Mrs. Rowley and Uncle Albert grinned like two well-fed foxes, then headed off to Katie's Kitchen as Hope said, "They set me up."

"Very nicely, too. What should we do now?"

"Plan the wedding, what else?" She nodded at the retreating couple. "Are *you* going to tell them no? Tell the man who raised you and cared for you that you won't plan *his* wedding? Tell the woman who gave me a place to live I won't plan *her* wedding?"

"That means we're together. Didn't think you'd want to have anything to do with me after what transpired between us yesterday."

She squared her shoulders. "Yesterday was a red-letter day. Not because you thought I left town, but because I finally, once and for all, closed my old dependent life and officially started a new one. Hope Stevens, independent woman. I like the sound of that. And you're still the protector of Paradise Creek and not going to give that up, and I wouldn't want you to. So, we're just two people living in the same town planning a wedding. We won't let this marriage get personal. Albert and Lettie are the ones getting married, not us.''

He shrugged and nodded his approval. ''You know, that was a very good speech. Direct, noninflammatory, politically correct. How long did it take you to put it together?''

She shrugged in return. ''Couple hours last night, just tossed the wedding part in at the end. Nice touch, don't you think?''

''Your father would be proud.''

She looked up at him. ''Guess we're back to staying out of each other's way. The only reason it didn't work last time was because the town locked us in jail and there were...results. We can't have results again.''

Clay didn't say anything for a moment. Probably remembering those results. She sure was.

She swallowed hard, trying *not* to remember. ''Being friends won't work. You and I can't ever just be friends. With us it's all or nothing.''

''Yeah. All or nothing. Can we do nothing and be together and plan the wedding?''

She exchanged looks with him that said *no way*. ''Do you have your citation book?''

''You going to order me to stay away from you?''

''Don't get excited.'' *Excited?* She was the one getting excited. Thinking about jail and the rowboat was enough to excite a corpse.

He pulled the book out of his back pocket and she

snatched it along with a pen from his front pocket and wrote.

"What are you doing?"

"Hold your shirt on." She imagined him with his shirt off. She imagined him with *her* shirt off. She scribbled faster. She tore out the pink sheet of the citation and handed it to him. "Here's what you take care of. Everyone brings a covered dish to the wedding in place of presents. Folding chairs from the school. Ruth Owens bakes the cake. Jake takes pictures. The kids pick wildflowers. I'll do clothes, bouquet, ceremony and honeymoon."

Clay nodded. "We'll rendezvous at noon on Sunday, an hour before the wedding to check everything. Until then, we don't need to see each other. Right?"

"That's the whole point." She turned and headed for The Gray. She needed to get started on this wedding. Finding a bridal gown, maid-of-honor dress, contacting the reverend, thinking about a honeymoon would keep her busy for the next four days…until the wedding. But what would happen at the wedding? The maid of honor and best man couldn't avoid each other for an entire afternoon.

Chapter Ten

Clay knew there had never been a more beautiful day for a wedding than this one. Or a more dismal best man. Not that he wasn't happy for Uncle Albert and Lettie, but because his relationship with Red was a disaster. Probably because there *was* no relationship.

Noontime sun warmed the earth and leaves fluttered to the ground, adding to the autumn carpet already there. He straightened his tie and checked his watch for the second time. Where was Red? Hell, he'd asked himself that question for the past four days. He wasn't supposed to, that was the agreement, but for some reason it kept popping into his head. *Where was she?*

"Clay?"

He turned and saw Red walking up the hill, smiling and waving to him. The breeze ruffled her long forest-green dress that shimmered when she moved. She'd braided her hair and pinned it up, weaving in ribbons that floated in the air. She carried some sort of golden, vintage silk bouquet that matched. A woodland goddess. He'd never seen a more beautiful woman, anytime, anywhere.

"Hi," she said, stopping beside him. She looked around. "Wow, you did a great job. Chairs in place, tables for the food, tablecloths, dishes."

"Mrs. Owens outdid herself on the cake and the kids made bouquets of leaves since the rain crushed the flowers. Where'd you find the dress?"

"At The Gray. Lettie had packed away her keepsakes from years ago in an old trunk. Isn't this dress wonderful? And the ribbons and flowers? Mabel found a dress for Lettie in a trunk she'd kept. Never thought trunks could be so much fun."

How could they stand here talking clothes and flowers and cake when all he wanted to do was take her in his arms and kiss her?

"My father's letting the newlyweds use his condo in Vail for a honeymoon, and he kicked in the plane tickets since Mrs. Rowley kept me from being homeless."

He cupped her chin. "You're…stunning."

She smiled up at him, her eyes sparkling. "So are you." She smoothed her hand over his lapel. "I think this is the first time I've seen you without your uniform." Her eyes darkened a shade. His insides melted into a giant hormonal blob.

She put the flowers on one of the tables. "Town's making a lot of progress getting back together."

Clay nodded, thinking *yeah, and we're not.* Frustration over this whole blasted mess with Red ate at him. "Enjoying that independence of yours?"

She arched her brow and jutted her chin. "As a matter of fact, I am. I'm opening my own business, *Hope For Something Special.* I'm renting a table at Katie's Kitchen from two to five every day. Customers meet me there, I buy them lunch and we plan their special events, wardrobes or whatever."

"People around here can't afford that."

"What I can save them on making a good purchase instead of a bad purchase will more than pay my fee and there are other towns to draw from on the Eastern Shore. Since Lettie and Albert plan on living in The Gray, I've taken a room over Katie's. I'll be close to my work."

Clay felt his eyes widen. "Above Katie's? Billy Jones lives there."

"He's the one who told me about the place. He's helping me paint it and he offered to do promo work for my business on his computer."

"*Like hell.* Doing promo work on *you,* is more like it."

"And what's that supposed to mean?"

Clay loosened his tie, suddenly feeling as if he were going to suffocate. "Billy Jones has had his eye on you since you hit town. I've seen the smiles, the winks."

"He's nice."

"He's a wolf in computer clothing."

"He's also a mechanic. Very versatile."

"Then he's a wolf in computer and mechanic clothing. He's after you."

"What's it to you?"

Clay stopped dead. "He's not good for you. Not right. He's probably after your money."

"That's not true and you know it."

Yeah, he did know it, but it was the only thing he could think of at the moment. Why couldn't he just say, "I don't give a tinker's damn who you go with"? The words just wouldn't come out. By all rights they should flow from his lips like carols from a church choir at Christmastime.

He spied Uncle Albert heading up the hill, walking with his bride-to-be. "We'll talk about this later."

"No, we won't."

Clay drew up beside his uncle and draped his arm over his shoulder. He watched Red link her arm through Lettie's as his uncle said, "You two look real good. Good enough to get married yourselves. Want to join us?"

"Red and I wouldn't dream of horning in on your special day."

"Damn shame if you ask me. You two don't realize what you're missing. Sometimes you have to take a chance." He exchanged looks with Mrs. Rowley. "Guess our little scheme to get you together didn't work, but we want to thank you all the same for putting on such a fine shindig."

Red smiled at Clay. "Our pleasure. Now, if I can steal the bride for a minute, I'll get her flowers."

Clay watched Lettie leave with Red, then said to his uncle, "How're you holding up as an almost married man?"

"Couldn't be happier. Third happiest day of my life."

Clay did a double take. "Third?"

"I'm lucky enough to have three best days in my life, just don't know what order they should go in." He held up his fingers and counted. "There's marrying Annabelle, and now marrying Lettie, and then there's the day you landed on my doorstep."

Uncle Albert reached into the pocket of his blue suit and pulled out a folded paper. "Deed to the house. The white clapboard's yours now, since I'll be living with Lettie in The Gray."

He put his hand on Clay's shoulder. "Lot of happy memories in that house, Clay. First with Annabelle, then when you came along. It's up to you to keep the memories going. I'm proud of you, couldn't love you more if you were my own son."

An elephant suddenly sat on Clay's chest as Uncle Albert took Clay's hand and placed the deed in his palm. "'May good fortune be yours and may your joys never end.'" He winked. "Read that on the back of a bottle of fine Irish whiskey. Been waiting years for the right time to use it."

Clay studied the deed. "I don't know what to say."

"Say that if you find another bottle of that whiskey you'll invite me over for a drink."

Clay hugged his uncle, the man who'd saved his butt so many years ago and taught him that being a man meant taking care of what's given to you.

He let his uncle go. "I'll miss you."

"I'll be two doors away, boy."

The elephant got a little heavier. "I'll miss you."

He pulled in a big breath and straightened his spine. "It's time for you to get married." He nodded toward town. "People are starting to arrive."

"Lettie and I need to be there to greet them." He turned from Clay and walked across the grass, meeting Lettie on the way. They held hands and greeted Doc and his wife as Jake and Carlie snapped pictures.

Red strode toward Clay. She looked…harried. "Have you seen Reverend Wilks? I haven't—"

Clay hitched his chin at two men talking as they came up the hill. "There. Don't panic."

"Easy for you to say, he was on *my* list." She nodded at the high school and elementary music teachers tuning their instruments. "I hope they're good."

The air suddenly filled with music and she smiled. "They *are* good."

Folks strolled up the hill and greeted Lettie and

Uncle Albert. Clay felt depressed as hell. He was losing Red and he couldn't think of a way to stop it, and even if he did stop it how would it ever work out? "Why don't you move in with me? Into the clapboard?"

Did he really say that? *Yes,* and it was a damn fine idea. "There's room. I won't even charge you rent."

She looked at him as if he'd sprouted another head. "What are you talking about?"

"You're moving in with Billy Jones. Why not move in with me? You take the top floor of the house, and I'll take the bottom. Put in a separate entrance to preserve that new independence you found and—"

"That was a patronizing crack, Clay Mitchell, and I don't appreciate it one bit. And I'm not moving in with Billy. He lives in one apartment and I live in the next, and moving in with you is not how to stay away from each other like we agreed. You *do* remember that conversation, don't you?"

Yeah, he remembered that conversation and was thinking about having his tongue surgically removed for agreeing to it. What had he been thinking?

She nodded to the front of the crowd. "It's showtime."

Everyone was seated and Reverend Wilks took his place. Clay and Uncle Albert took theirs. The music swelled and Red walked slowly down the isle. He watched her every step, wondering what it would be like to have her in his life on a permanent basis. Then he pushed away his problems and concentrated on the words that united Lettie and Uncle Albert as husband and wife. He didn't look at Red. To be near her yet so far away was torture.

At the end of the ceremony, everyone cheered the happy couple and the musicians played a song about love being lovelier the second time around. He looked at Red as she watched the dancing. It was the second time around for them, too. Why couldn't it be lovelier for them like it was for Albert and Lettie?

Red came to him. "They want us to join them." She nodded at the dance floor.

"This isn't helping us stay apart."

"And having me move in with you will?"

"Let's dance." Did she have to feel so perfect in his arms? Feel as if she belonged there?

"You stepped on my toe."

"Think of it as helping to keep us apart. Whatever you do, don't catch the bouquet."

"And you don't catch the garter. We'll get Carlie and Jake to do the honors. Get us out of the spotlight and them in."

Truth be told, Clay was thrilled to see the happy couple finally on their way and the last of the guests meander back to town. He was beat. Trying to stay away from Red when the whole town was hellbent on getting them together was hard work. He snapped the garter on his sleeve. The town won.

He undid the top button of his dress shirt, his tie

already loose around his neck, and began folding the chairs he and Sam had set up that morning. Sam pulled his pickup beside Clay and got out. "What a day."

"And then some."

Sam stuffed his tie in his pocket as he surveyed the aftermath of the wedding. "*If,* and I do mean *if,* I ever get hitched, I'm having one of those casual weddings. No suits and no ties, 'course I wouldn't do anything without asking Red's opinion first. She knows how to make everything just perfect no matter what kind of affair you're throwing."

Clay stopped folding and looked at Sam. "Married? You? A card-carrying member of bachelors-are-us?"

Sam let loose with a laugh and ran his hand through his hair that had been plastered neat for the occasion. "Don't go getting any ideas. I said *if.* The way I see it, you and Red should be getting hitched next." He eyed the garter. "Then Jake and Carlie. I'm just in the looking stage."

"Didn't know you were in any stage."

"A man's always in a stage, Clay."

Clay studied Sam. Something was different. Clay folded another chair and swung it onto the stack of chairs already on the truck. "Jake and Carlie look like a sure bet, but I wouldn't be giving odds for me and Red."

He cast a quick glance to where Uncle Albert and

Lettie had married a few hours ago and where Red was now helping Ruth Owens box up the rest of the wedding cake.

Sam nudged Clay. "Instead of scorching the landscape with those hot looks you two give each other all the time, why don't you do something about it? Elope."

Clay laughed. "That's for sure not going to happen. There're complications."

"I got a news flash for you, Sheriff, old boy. When it comes to women there're always complications, but the big question is, do you love her? Once you decide if you do or don't, then everything sort of falls into place."

Clay snatched a chair from Sam's hand and looked him straight in the eyes. "Okay, what's gotten into you? How do you know all this? You've never been married, never even talked about it, until today."

Sam shuffled his feet. "I've been reading."

"Reading what?"

Sam reddened from his chin to his forehead. "Romance novels, if you have to be so galdern nosy. That night the electric was knocked out I couldn't watch TV. Ruth was helping out at the gym when I stopped by. Gave me one of her romance books. I figured it was better than pacing and wearing out good shoe leather and there wasn't anything else to do at that point but listen to rain. I was really getting tired of that rain."

He reddened a bit more, but pushed on. "Wouldn't harm you none to be reading them, either, even if the electric is back on or not. Made me realize none of us lives forever and life's precious and a million times better when you share it with someone. So there, Clay Mitchell, I said it and proud I did."

Sam snatched up a chair and tossed it into his pickup. He winked at Ruth. *Huh? Sam wink? At Ruth Owens? What the heck was that all about?*

Clay said, "Tell me this, is the whole blamed town in love? Jake? You? Ruth? Carlie?" *Billy Jones?* Damn. "Anyone I'm missing here?"

Sam grinned and there was a spark in his eye. "I got a feeling that when springtime comes around, Paradise Creek is going to have a real rush on weddings and a bit of a baby boom. Nothing like almost losing the things you cherish most in this world to make a person see what's really important. Plus, the electricity was out."

He flashed a devilish grin. "Gotta do something when the electricity's out and sleep isn't always the answer."

Clay watched as Sam levered himself into his pickup and drove off toward Ruth and Red. Ruth laughed like a schoolgirl as the truck came her way. Then she opened the passenger side and hopped in beside Sam. Laughter bubbled from the truck, then it took off bumping over the uneven ground toward the road heading for town.

Red seemed to be as mesmerized by Ruth and Sam's antics as he was. She continued to watch the truck while she walked over to him. It wasn't a walk, he decided, keeping his eyes on her. Red sort of floated in a sea of dark green.

When she got to him she said, "Can you fit the last two folding tables in your cruiser and give me a lift into town? Ruth and Sam drove off before I could put the tables on top of the chairs." She glanced to the retreating truck as it bounced over the grass till it got to the road. "I don't think those two had tables on their minds."

She smelled of wildflowers and fresh air. How was he supposed to stay away from that? "Don't have my cruiser. I walked up like everyone else. If you can carry the cake, I can handle the tables. They're aluminum with carrying handles on the sides when they're closed up."

The sun was setting now a half sphere perched on the horizon, the chill of autumn replacing the warmth of late summer. Clay took off his coat and draped it around Red's shoulders. He realized the thing he missed most between him and Red was the sharing, whether it was his coat or his chicken or laughter. He'd miss that even more than the sex, and that was saying one hell of a lot.

No one could read him the way Red could. She knew when he was happy or sad or worried. And when he was worried she tried to help. No one else had ever seen into his heart the way she did. No one had ever touched him with one look, one word, one simple kiss.

"Now you'll be cold."

Just looking at her made him anything but cold. "I'm fine."

She put Lettie's bouquet, which she had caught after all, on top of the cake box as he collapsed one table, then the other. "I would have thought with all the people here there wouldn't be any cake left."

"This is the top layer. I'm going to freeze it, and then on Albert and Lettie's first anniversary, they can defrost it and celebrate all over again. It's what I would have liked to do with my own wedding cake, *if* there had been a wedding."

He picked up one table in each hand, carrying them like suitcases. He and Red started down the road, walking past the old church. "Do you wish there had been a wedding?" He had no right to ask, but he wanted to know. Did she miss Kenneth? Regret not living the glamorous life?

"I regret not getting the cake. White chocolate, butter icing. Food to die for."

Clay chuckled, as the serenity of early evening settled in around them. A morning dove called, animals scurried in the brush, Red's dress swished as she walked beside him. The thought of her never walking beside him again made his insides ache as if he had the flu and his heart hurt as if someone were tearing it out of his chest. It was a hell of a way to feel. A hell of a way to live.

"Let's take the shortcut through the woods. That's the way I came here when I helped Bobby off the church roof, and it's getting late."

Did she have to remind him of how she helped the town? Did she have to be so damn beautiful? He needed to put Red out of his mind before he lost it completely. It had been a long and tedious day. It was time to put it behind him. He picked up the pace and headed into the woods.

"Hey, slow down a little. I'm not wearing hiking boots, you know."

He tramped around the corner and down the path. He nearly slid on the thick carpet of leaves, but he hurried anyway. He heard her dress rustling behind him but refused to look back, because if he did, if he caught one more look at her, they'd never get out of these damn woods till morning and that was a conservative estimate.

She said, "I don't remember there being so many rocks and leaves the last time—*yikes!*"

Clay spun around in time to see Red slide on the leaves, trip over a root and land headfirst behind a bush. He let go of the tables, ran toward her and dropped to his knees beside her. "Are you okay?"

He pulled her up by her shoulders, then tipped her head back, stealing himself against her sparkling eyes, creamy skin, incredible fragrance and…and icing smeared face?

He helped her sit down on a log. "Well, it could have been worse. The icing's only on your cheek and your chin and your nose. And a little bit on your ear."

She raised one icing covered brow. "How could it have been worse?"

He shrugged. "It could have gotten on my coat."

He wiped her chin with his index finger and licked it. "If it's any consolation, you taste very good."

He watched a smile pull at her lips. Then she scooped a dollop of cake from her chin, licked it and started to laugh, making him laugh right along with her. "I shouldn't laugh. I ruined Albert and Lettie's anniversary cake." She picked up the bouquet. "Flattened."

"You can press the flowers and Ruth can make another top layer before they get home. Sometimes a white lie isn't so bad."

"A sheriff lying? My, my."

He took his handkerchief from his pocket and cleaned off her nose. She wiped a smear of icing from the corner of her mouth and slowly, then provocatively, put her thumb into his mouth. Their eyes locked as he licked, tasting the warm sweetness of the cake and Red and all the good things between them. Then he kissed her and all their problems didn't seem nearly so important as the two of them together right now.

He framed her face with his palms and deepened the kiss as his lips formed to hers. Their tongues mingled, propositioned…then promised. He heaved a mental sigh of fulfillment and leaned forward, taking her into his arms, wanting to feel her body next to his. She swayed, grabbed his shirt and yelped as they toppled backwards over the log.

They were chest to chest, his legs straddling her middle; their eyes, nose, lips in perfect alignment. Her eyes twinkled, her cheeks were pink with vitality. He looked at her full, rich, tempting lips. "It's a sign. I'm supposed to make love to you here in the woods."

"I think it's a sign that we're not supposed to be in these woods."

He kissed her forehead. "I like my interpretation better."

"It won't help us stay apart."

"Will anything?"

"A lobotomy."

He laughed and rolled over, taking her with him. Her laughter mixed with his as she landed on top of him. Then her laughter gave way to a sexy smile. She fiddled with a button on his shirt. "I have a confession. I've wanted to see you without clothes since I wrecked Delia's van and fell into your arms."

She undid one shirt button and his heart slid right into his stomach. She undid the rest, then ran her hands over his chest, making pleasure roar through him like a freight train out of control. She pushed his shirt to his sides and he jumped.

She grinned. "Ticklish?"

"Don't even think what you're thinking, Red."

"Lucky for you I'm preoccupied with other things at the moment." She trailed her fingers slowly down his middle, leaving a path of fire in her wake. She stopped at his belt. "You are magnificent, even more than I imagined." Her eyes filled with satisfaction, her voice a whisper. "Am I making you uncomfortable?"

"Anyone but you, yes. But not with you."

She gave him a wicked grin and undid his buckle, then unzipped his pants.

"I have only so much self-control."

He made to snatch her wrist and bring her close, but she dodged him. "Patience is a virtue."

"Not now." And he turned over, putting her underneath him. He straddled her, memorizing the laughter in her eyes and on her lips, then he slowly inched up her dress, revealing... "A black garter belt?"

"It fit with the dress. Classic."

"Sexy."

"That, too."

He gave her an even look. "You anticipated this?"

"I like feeling sexy when you're around."

His heart raced and he kissed her. Then he undid the garters and slowly slid off her stockings one at a time, draping them over his shoulders. He took off the black slip of sexy lace, then her panties. "You are so beautiful."

He touched her, needing to feel the soft curls hiding her soft intimate secrets. Her breath quickened, her eyes clouded with passion and his fingers slid deeper, separating her, stroking her, pleasing her.

"Clay?" She held out her arms to him and he settled himself over her. Then she wrapped her legs around him and he was inside of her, filling her, climaxing with her.

Was this the last time he'd ever make love to Red? The last time his name would be on her lips in the heat of passion? How could he live with that?

IT HAD TO BE MONDAY, Clay decided as he glanced at the early morning sun hiding behind a puff of clouds. Everything was always nuts on Monday, and since he was pinning documents to a clothesline outside the courthouse office, this one was no different.

Clay heard Jake's cruiser pull up next to the curb, the engine die, door slam and Jake ask, "What in the Sam Hill are you doing, clothespinning papers from one end of the courthouse to the other?"

"Drying out old records before they get moldy. The flood drenched the bottom two file cabinet drawers in our office and they held these papers that have never been put on the computer. I can't just pitch them."

Clay reached for another report—this one by Sheriff Page, dated 1968, for breaking up a barroom fight and tossing five men in jail. Sheriff Page was no wimp. Clay snapped the report to the clothesline.

"You look like hell. Did you know Red's moving into an apartment over Katie's? And that Billy Jones lives across the hall?"

He ground his teeth and swore.

"I'll take that for a yes. What are you going to do about it?"

Clay stopped pinning. "What can I do about it?"

Jake shrugged. "Hell if I know. She's your gal."

"She is not my gal." But he wanted her to be.

"If you want to pin up old documents instead of chase Red, that's your business. Think I'll drive on out along Little Creek and see how the folks there are getting on with repairs. The hardware store will be needing to deliver supplies up that way and I can take some with me."

Clay clipped another report. Sheriff Simmons, 1979, for a robbery at the grocery store. Captured two men on the "Most Wanted" list. Simmons wasn't any wimpy sheriff, either. "Going to take Carlie Lewis along?"

"Well now, why didn't I think of that, especially since she doesn't have to be at the drugstore until noon. Think I'll stop by the post office on the way back and see if my new jacket's in. Red helped me pick it out. On sale, too. The woman's a wonder, don't know how I'd get along without her." He leveled Clay a look. "The question is, how are you going to get along without her?"

Clay jabbed the next document onto the line. "Fine. Just fine."

"Any more fine and you'll rupture something."

Clay watched Jake get back into the cruiser and pull away. It wasn't that he found Jake's driving so interesting, but what he said was worth thinking about. Clay stroked his chin. It *was* his funeral because the one person he cared most about was not a part of his life and he didn't want to get along without her.

He thought about all they'd been through together. How having her with him during the flood meant more to him than anything else. He'd never met a woman as strong and courageous and selfless and supportive as Red.

He respected her for having the guts to change her life and stick around when things got tough. He liked being with her, and that's why he acted like an ass when he thought she'd left. Would he have made love to her every chance he had if he didn't want her in his life?

Okay, he wanted her in his life, now he had to figure out how to get her there.

He picked up another sheriff's report—Sheriff Casey Malone, 1972, for driving a motorcycle gang out of town. Malone must have been one persuasive guy. A sheriff not to mess with.

Clay stopped for a moment and looked at all the sheriff reports fluttering in the breeze and suddenly realized what he had to do. There was a way to keep Red in his life. It would cost him a lot, but it couldn't be any more painful than losing Red.

Chapter Eleven

Hope walked into the sheriff's office with Clay's coat over her arm.

"Hi, Jake. Is Clay in the back room? I want to return this to him. Just got it back from the cleaners."

"Grass stains. Everybody knows." He threw his pencil onto the desk and scowled.

"Hey, they came out. No need to get upset." The gossip network had struck again.

"It's not the stains and Clay's not in the back. And since you even asked where he is I'm assuming you've been living on the moon all morning. Town's in a real tizzy over where Clay Mitchell *is* and where he *should* be."

"I've been up at Willow Pond Church taking measurements and pictures to get the papers filled out for The National Register of Historic Places. Why are you sitting at Clay's desk? And why are you buried behind so much paperwork? I thought Clay took care of most of that. What's going on?"

Jake's expression was pained. "Clay resigned. He's not sheriff of Paradise Creek anymore. He went and left me in charge. Why he thought I'd want to be in charge, I'll never know."

She sat down in one of the wooden chairs and steadied her head with her hand. "Wh—what do you mean, Clay's not sheriff?"

"Said he needed to mellow out."

"This *is* Sheriff Clay Mitchell of Paradise Creek we're talking about?"

"The one and only, except he isn't sheriff anymore. Sam and I and everyone else tried to talk him out of quitting but got nowhere. He's down by the docks, fishing. Hard to imagine he knows which end of the fishing pole to hold on to and which gets the line."

"I don't get it."

Jake spread his hands palms-up. "Neither does anyone else. He did say something about not really deserving to be sheriff anymore, whatever that means. He just got this town through a flood and now he thinks he shouldn't be sheriff? I can't imagine where that came from."

Jake shook his head, then glared at the paperwork. "I have a dinner date with Carlie. I don't want to miss that, and my new coat came in and I planned on wearing it. Now I—"

"Did you call Doc? Maybe Clay's sick. Why

would he give up being sheriff? Everyone knows it's the only thing he's ever wanted to do."

Jake groused, "Apparently not. Apparently there's something else sticking in his craw that we don't know about. Talk to him. See if you can straighten him out and do it fast. I'm a deputy. I don't mind taking a few classes now and then to be a better one, but I'm not a sheriff and don't want to be one."

On her way to the docks, Hope stopped at Katie's for two turkey club sandwiches to go. Sam, Mabel, Ruth and Katie had no idea what was going on with Clay, either. *Mystery at Paradise Creek*. But she didn't think anything she'd learned from Nancy Drew would help her out this time.

She got the sandwiches and made her way to the docks where she spied Clay sitting cross-legged at the end, messing with a fishing pole.

He had on…jeans? And a denim jacket? Was that a baseball cap? Didn't his closet consist of khaki uniform, khaki uniform, khaki uniform?

"What in the world are you doing?" she asked as she drew up beside him.

He gave her a lazy look and yawned. He looked back to the Bay as gulls skimmed the surface. "Fishing?"

"Do you know how?"

He eyed the brown bags. "I smell lunch."

He put down the pole and she handed him the bag.

"Why did you resign from being sheriff? Why didn't you tell me you were going to do this?"

"It was kind of sudden. Like three hours ago."

"And why isn't half the town here trying to talk you out of it?"

"The whole town already tried. But I'm not listening." He peered into one bag and pulled out one sandwich. He slowly unwrapped it.

Slowly? He never did anything slow. "Do you know I passed two cars parked illegally on my way down here and there was no ticket on either of them? And then I noticed a truck on Main Street with expired tags and a broken windshield. How safe it that?"

"Good sandwich."

She threw her hands in the air. "How can you just sit here? Whatever happened about this being *your* town? For heaven's sake, do something."

She thought he hesitated a moment before he took another bite. "Don't suppose you brought any spicy mustard to go with this?"

Hope yanked the sandwich from his fingers and glared at him. "All right, that's it. What's gotten into you?"

"You."

She shook her head, trying to clear her thoughts. "What do I have to do with your decision to give up being sheriff? I can't even imagine."

"You don't like me bossy and arrogant and dictatorial, right? Well, sheriffs are all that and a whole lot more. All the things you're trying to get away from, they excel in. That includes me. I want you in my life. If I'm sheriff it's not going to happen."

"It's not the uniform that makes you bossy, it's you. A genetic thing or whatever. It's not because you wear khaki with a badge."

"Being sheriff is a big part of it because it's my life. Thought I'd try and get a new one."

"You gave up being sheriff because of me?"

"Bingo."

"Everyone's going to run me out of here. They'll hate me and I don't blame them. And you're going to be miserable."

"No I won't." He held up his fishing pole with line tangled around it.

"Some substitute for being sheriff."

"Jake will take care of everything. He hired a deputy from Chestertown."

"Jake isn't you. You're the one who takes care of everything around here and everyone knows it. You can't quit."

He shrugged.

She ran her hand through her hair and took in a steadying breath. "You did this so we could be together?"

"Least have a stab at it."

His look was as sincere as the stature of Lincoln at the Memorial as he continued, "I don't expect you to go back to being go-with-the-flow Red. Fact is I've never known you that way and I like you just the way you are. If we want to find out if there's anything between us, I can't be sheriff. Can I have my sandwich back now?''

She returned his lunch. ''You're willing to give up being sheriff for…me?''

''You called your dad and gave up your personal plans to help Paradise Creek and to help me.'' His fingers closed over hers. ''We have a lot going for us. I don't want to lose that. I don't want to lose you.''

She tried to speak but words wouldn't come. He did all this for her? He wanted them to be together more than anything, even more than being sheriff?

She sat down beside him and framed his face with her hands. ''You can't do this, Clay. It's a really bad idea. You'll go nuts, you'll drive us all nuts. The whole town will go on antidepressants.''

''Let's go to Lickity's tonight. They're having a *We Fooled The Flood* party, serving Rocky Road ice cream and some dessert called *Dirt and Worms*. Meet me there at seven. I have to check out an oyster boat. I'm thinking about being an oyster man like Uncle Albert. If it's good enough for him, it's fine for me. Terrific idea, don't you think?''

''You're asking me what you should do?''

''See, I'm changing already.''

''Oysters?''

"It'll be an exciting career change."

She waved her hand at the Bay and the boats at the dock. "It'll be suicide. Some morning your poor sorry carcass will wash up on the shore. It'll give Paradise Creek a bad name."

He cupped the back of her head with his right hand and kissed her. "I'm going to be just what you want me to be. A regular guy. No ordering you or anyone else around. That's all in the past, Hope."

"Hope? What happened to Red?"

"Red was part of our old life together, this is the beginning of something new for us."

"But… But…" She stared at Clay. "This is all wrong."

"It's all right. It's what you wanted and it's fine with me. I'll meet you at seven at Lickity's. Order whatever you want. We can share. Do you know what time it is?"

"You want me to order for you? And what have you done with your watch?"

"At home in a drawer with my star. Don't need either of them anymore."

She had that same feeling as when she rode roller coasters after eating a big lunch. It's what she wanted but suddenly not what she wanted. "It's a little after two. There's something else, why did you tell Jake you didn't deserve to be sheriff? What was that all about?"

"Doesn't matter because I'm not sheriff."

And she believed him. He looked totally…placid. Placid and Clay Mitchell in the same sentence was unnatural. The new Clay Mitchell was charming as a Southern gentleman, cordial as a handshake and it all felt as out of place as a mouse in a meat loaf.

"I have to go. I promised Katie I'd help her unpack the new dishes and glassware she and I ordered. Yellow and blue stripes, very chic." She stood.

"See you at Lickity's. No emergencies to interrupt, no sheriff responsibilities to get in our way. Just us. Just what you want."

CLAY WATCHED RED walk away from the marina as Sam approached and said. "Well, have you changed your mind, yet? Red convince you to be sheriff around here like you're supposed to be and stop all this nonsense?"

"Jake's the sheriff." Clay picked up the fishing rod and the spool of line, then freed the innocent worms he couldn't spear onto a hook no matter how long he sat on the end of this damn dock. He snatched up his hat, stuffed it in his back pocket, then tossed his sandwich to the fishes. He wasn't hungry.

Sam shook his head. "Heard you're taking up oystering. Where'd that idea come from?"

He tried to concentrate on the oyster boat he had an appointment to see at five, but all that came to mind were two illegally parked cars and a truck that had expired tags and a cracked windshield.

"Either you've fallen asleep with your eyes wide open, or you're rethinking this oyster idea and that's the smartest thing you've done all day. All you know about oysters is how to eat them."

Clay headed up the gravel drive with Sam in tow. Mrs. Farley called from her front porch, "Clay, that dog across the way's barking all the time again. Can you take care of it?"

"Call Jake. He's the sheriff now, you know."

Mrs. Farley wagged her finger. "Hogwash. That's what this resignation of your is, hogwash." She glared at Clay for a moment, then slammed her door shut.

"Things aren't working out quite the way you thought they would, are they? Bet you thought Jake would just love being sheriff and the good citizens would support him and all would be well."

Clay spied one of the cars that was double-parked and Sam said, "Look at this. Makes a sheriff, even an ex-sheriff want to whip out a pad and write a ticket doesn't it?"

"Furthest thing from my mind."

"You'll need an SA group, Sheriffs Anonymous for used-to-be sheriffs who can't give up the job."

Clay turned to Sam. "Go oil your backhoe or visit with Ruth Owens for a spell."

"You're just cranky 'cause you know I'm right."

Clay watched Sam head for Ruth's house, then he turned for the courthouse as if pulled in that direction by some huge magnet. Who was he kidding? He wanted to see how things were going.

He walked up the steps reminding himself he was an outsider now, just another citizen in the courthouse there for a little visit. He'd taped over his own name on the Sheriff's Office door and wrote Jake's in its place. He eyed the tape. He'd get used to his name not being there. Someday. Just not today.

As he entered Jake said, "Back for your job? 'Bout time."

Clay studied his desk, rather the desk that had been his. He'd stripped off the white paint and refinished it to a fine old oak luster. It was a great desk, what he could see of it. Papers were strewn about, pencils were half-chewed and there was a coffee cup sitting on the wood without anything under it for protection.

"Heard you were buying a boat." The phone rang and Jake answered it. As Jake went to the file cabinets to get some information, Clay snatched up the cup, used his shirtsleeve to wipe the ring, then grabbed a paper from the waste can, folded it and put under the cup. The computer was on, an unfinished state report on the monitor. Due today. Clay finished the report, stacked up papers, put the pencils in the holder, then sat down in the chair on the non-business side of the desk as Jake came back.

He growled, "So, what do you want?"

"To see how you're doing."

Jake yanked the star from his chest and slid it

across the desk. "Take it and I'll be doing fine. I don't cotton to all this responsibility, Clay."

He shoved his hands in his pockets and thought of Red to keep himself from reaching for the star. He wondered if Jake had sent over the weekly report to the town council yet. "What I'm trying to do is give Red and me a fresh start. I can't be sheriff."

Had Jake laid out the route for the Halloween Parade next week? There wouldn't be a fair but the parade was still on. Did Jake remember that? Did he remember to order the candy to hand out to the kids? And there were three faxes lying in the tray that needed checking.

Jake propped his feet on the desk and Clay ground his teeth. Jake said, "You are who you are, Clay, and you're the sheriff. You can't change."

"I will change." He stood and put a paper under Jake's feet. "Just stand back and watch me. I'm a new man, dammit, and getting newer by the day, and I couldn't be any flipping happier if I was a hyena."

Clay stomped out of the office, stomped down the hall, and slammed the courthouse door behind him absolutely delirious with happiness.

HOPE SAT AT THE RED vinyl-upholstered booth at Lickity Splits and listened as Elvis told her she was a hound dog and no friend of his. Elvis was half-right. She may not be a hound dog, but she certainly wasn't a friend to him or anyone else in this town until she got Clay Mitchell back as sheriff. And if her little scheme worked, he'd have a star back on his chest in—she checked her watch—less than an hour.

She waved at Sam and Ruth. They gave her a knowing nod. Others in the jam-packed ice-cream shop stopped by to say hi and let her know they'd all gotten the message, thanks to the Paradise Creek gossips. Operation Sheriff Clay Mitchell was in full swing.

She flipped through the jukebox selection perched at the end of the table. She didn't like tricking Clay, but there was no other way. She couldn't live with herself if he gave up the job he loved more than anything just to be with her. What kind of happiness could come from that? But he wasn't listening to her or anyone else.

She waved at Clay as he came in the door and walked her way. He was still dressed in jeans and jacket. No hat this time, and that was an improvement. A baseball hat on Clay worked about as well as a tiara on a thoroughbred. She looked at his garb and decided none of it worked. He looked as comfortable in regular clothes as she did in billowing pink chiffon.

He slid in the bench opposite her and she asked, ''How'd oyster boat buying go?''

He put his elbows on the table and leaned forward. ''There are two kids smoking behind Sam's welding shed. Saw them on my way here.'' Clay cracked his knuckles.

''Sam's shed isn't on the way to anywhere.''

''I was…taking a walk.''

Like you used to do when you were sheriff, she added to herself, confirming her decision was the right one.

''I can't call Jake because he's having dinner with Carlie over in Rockhall and I can't find our new deputy anywhere. Those kids shouldn't be smoking. I could just tell their parents but, but…''

Clay suddenly smiled. It looked forced. He leaned back but didn't look comfortable. ''None of this is my problem, is it?'' He glanced around. ''It's all adults here tonight. Where are the kids?''

''Parents night out. Kids are at the high school watching movies.''

''I checked out the boat, and it's great. We can take it for a test drive tomorrow. We can pack a picnic lunch, motor on over to Rockhall. What do you think of that? Can't remember the last picnic I was on.''

She glanced at her watch. ''Wonderful, terrific.''

''Going somewhere?'' He nodded at her wrist.

''No, of course not.''

There was a screech of tires outside the shop followed by a crash of metal against metal. The sound of cars crunching together and it was right on time. Being in Paradise Creek, she'd almost forgotten what a car crash sounded like.

Clay bolted upright and looked out the plate glass window. "It's the Jones brothers and some of the troublemakers from the next town over."

He made for the door along with everyone else at Lickity's and Red followed. The driver of the scrunched pickup and his friend climbed out of the truck, yelling and swearing, and the Jones brothers did the same. The four got closer, nose-to-nose, louder.

Ruth Owens and Sam pulled up beside Clay and said, "You better do something fast. There's going to be a fight. I know those two in the pickup and they go around just sniffing for trouble. 'Course the Jones boys aren't exactly known for their diplomacy skills, either. You best make all of them understand there's no fighting in this town, Clay. We don't need a reputation that allows for fighting in the streets or we'll have more problems than we can handle."

Clay's lips drew into a straight line. "I can't do anything. I'm not the sheriff anymore. Go call the new deputy."

Ruth said, "No one knows where he is. Doesn't answer his dispatch. Haven't seen him all evening. Worthless as a bucket of spit, if you ask me."

Was that smoke curling from Clay's ears? *Good.* Very good. He took a deep breath and said, "Well, somebody better go find him and do it now. We need someone with authority."

Ruth said, "That used to be you, Clay Mitchell. Before you went and quit on us."

Cars stopped to see what all the commotion was about except someone didn't stop fast enough and back-ended another car. Was this part of the original plan? The Jones brothers seemed a little shocked as drivers jumped out of the other cars and began shouting. Then Hope caught sight of a fist connecting to an eye. Uh-oh.

Clay pulled Hope and Ruth Owens out of harms way. Clay said to Sam, "Find that damn deputy and tell him if he knows what's good for him he better get…"

Clay's words trailed off. These were idle threats. More fists connected to their marks. Hope said to Clay, "The whole town's going to end up in a brawl."

"Stay put. Understand? Don't move."

He elbowed his way into the middle of the fighting and stood in the bed of the pickup truck. She could tell he was calling for the fighting to stop until someone climbed into the truck with Clay, had some words, then landed a fist right in his jaw.

What had she done? This was supposed to be a little scuffle, some pushing and shoving. No one got hurt, more show than fists, so Clay would realize he was needed. Now Clay was in an impossible situation. She was an idiot. Thanks to her, Clay had no authority, no badge, not even his bullhorn and a full-scale fistfight on his hands. Some might even take a fancy to punching out an ex-sheriff. Was this any way to treat the man she loved?

Loved? Did she love Clay? She watched him pull two fighters apart. Oh hell, of course she loved him. She wouldn't be worried into a cold sweat at the moment or trying to orchestrate his return to sheriff if she didn't love him. She wouldn't be making deals with the powers-that-be to let Clay be all right if she didn't love him in the first place. How was she going to get him out of this?

Chapter Twelve

Clay dodged a well-aimed punch and looked up in time to see Red grab Ruth Owens's purse, swing the big black leather bag around and land it firmly against the back of a troublemaker's head. The burly guy stumbled, turned, glared at Red, then shoved her hard, knocking her to the street on her finely shaped hind end.

Anger snapped through Clay like a crack of lightning and he made his way toward the man who'd dared to touch Red. Clay spun him around and did a fast one-two, knocking the guy flat on his back, giving him the sky to stare at while contemplating his wrongdoing.

A rumbling sound and the scent of diesel fumes drew Clay's attention up the street. Sam and his trusty backhoe were heading right for the middle of the fight, sending fighting men and Red running. The Jones brothers gave Sam a little salute of *thanks for helping out* as the backhoe stopped inches from the wrecked cars.

Sam killed the engine as Clay yelled, "Fight's over. Everybody go home."

Frustration tightened his chest as he considered how little he could do to break up the fight because he wasn't sheriff. He had to rely on Sam's backhoe of all things. He wasn't used to relying on anything but himself.

Someone in the crowd yelled back, "This is all your fault, Clay Mitchell. If you were sheriff nobody would dare fight in this town. You would have put an end to it before it started. This town's never been in such sorry shape and it's all your doin'."

Clay put his hands to his hips. "Now you listen up, all of you. You have a good sheriff. Jake. He's a fine man. None better."

Mabel Farley said, "You're the sheriff. That's why we elected you and that's what we expect you to be. Fact is, that's why we're all here in the first place, so you'd wake up and realize it, too."

Everyone went dead quiet. Clay said in a too calm voice, "*Why* are you all here?"

The crowd parted as Red made her way to him. "This whole thing is my idea, my fault. Everything got out of hand." She turned to the crowd. "I'm sorry."

Ruth said, "As long as Clay gets back to being

sheriff it's all worth it. You were just trying to help, so there's nothing to be sorry about.''

The crowd nodded and Clay narrowed his eyes and glared at Red. ''We need to talk.''

Mabel said, ''Don't you go giving her a hard time, Clay Mitchell, when you're the one needing a talking to.''

Clay put on his best sheriff's face. ''This has gone far enough. Everyone go home.''

''You're not the sheriff. You can't tell us what to do.''

''*Go.*''

The crowd muttered, then dispersed, some going home, most going back into the malt shop. He snagged Red's arm before she could join in the exodus. ''Not you.''

She shrugged. ''It was worth a try.''

He gave orders on unscrambling the cars and clearing the streets. When the last car hobbled away, he walked to Red, sitting on the edge of the sidewalk. ''What the hell did you do?''

She stood and dusted off her slacks and he said, ''Let's walk. We have an audience.'' He nodded at Lickity's.

''It's Paradise Creek. There's always an audience.''

''Tell me about the fight.''

''You're not going to like it. I was trying to save you from yourself.''

''What book did you get that out of?''

"It's the truth. You need to be sheriff."

"Since you got here, all I've heard is how I'm too bossy. I change and you don't like that, either?"

She stopped in the middle of the street. "I don't want you to be something you're not. You need to be a sheriff. That's who you are and tonight was a bad attempt on my part to get you to realize it."

He growled. "You risked someone getting hurt to prove to me that I need to be sheriff?"

She put her hands on her hips. "It was a good plan until that other accident happened. The Jones brothers staged all this and there was just supposed to be some yelling and shoving and you were supposed to see that it was your duty to be sheriff and put an end to such things."

"And how much did all this cost you?"

"Not much."

He quirked his brow.

"Billy Jones helped me come up with the plan when we were settling up for the repairs on Delia's van."

"So, it's Billy again."

"I paid for the damaged cars, which were just wrecks to begin with and any fines if it came to that. And, yes, Billy is a friend and if you don't approve, that's your problem."

"What would you ever do without your bank account?"

"I was just trying to get you to realize you need to be sheriff."

"Because I don't have a superior education like you? So how could I ever know what's best for myself."

"What's wrong with you? Don't you get it? I love you. That's why I did all this. I fell in love with you as a sheriff. It's who you are. I don't want you to be anything else. I want us to get married and have a family and you to be sheriff."

"You love me?"

"Yes." She spread her arms wide. "Would I have done all this if I didn't?"

"What happened to that independence you're so worried about?"

"Look at me. I'm independent, and we may fight like cats and dogs but I seem to be holding my own."

"It won't work. Not you and me."

She looked stricken and he hated himself for that. But it was the truth.

"You don't love me, do you?"

"Look at us. There's not one thing in common. You're used to having a big bank account to get what you want. That's what you just did. How could you be happy with a small-town sheriff? In a small town? It's boring."

"In case you haven't noticed, I spent the money on you, to make you happy. And I make things happen, I don't wait around for someone or someplace to entertain me. I may not be a know-it-all sheriff, but as a first-class volunteer I can assess what needs to be done and do it. If you loved me, you'd see that."

She stiffened her backbone. "Obviously, Clay Mitchell, you don't love me at all. You don't even know who I am."

Then she turned and walked away, leaving him in the middle of the street. Alone.

DAWN HAD BARELY chased away the night as Clay forced his tired body to jog up the sidewalk toward the courthouse. Dew still clung to the grass and a biting chill hinted at a hard frost. He watched as Jake balanced two jelly doughnuts on top of a cup of coffee and opened the door to the courthouse.

It was a study in perfection. Not a drop of coffee lost or a crumb of strawberry filled doughnut wasted. But right now Clay wasn't interested in Jake's juggling ability so much as the fact he was the sheriff of Paradise Creek and had all the legal clout of the office behind him.

"I need your help," Clay said as he followed Jake into the courthouse.

"Ever hear of wishing someone good morning before you go asking for favors?" He glanced at Clay. "What happened to you? You look like something the cat dragged in."

"Where have you been? And where was that no-good new deputy you hired when we needed him last night?''

"Never hired the deputy. Hoped you'd come to your senses. From the sounds of what happened last night, you didn't come to anything of the sort.''

"Where were *you* all night?''

"Willow Pond Church. Watched the sun come up with Carlie.''

"You were out all night and I can't keep track of Red for anything.''

"And I look great and you look like roadkill.'' Jake's grin split his face in two and he gave Clay a man-to-man wink. "Some of us got it, Clay, and some of us are too bullheaded to get anything. Mind opening the office door?''

Clay took the keys from Jake's fingers and undid the lock and flipped the lights. "I need you to put out a missing person bulletin right away. Red's gone. Vanished.'' Clay ran his hand through his hair. "I've been up all night looking for her everywhere. There was a fight on Main Street.''

"Heard all about it. Sure would have liked to see Red smack that guy with Ruth's purse.''

"I'm worried he might have come after her. She wasn't in The Gray last night. Even checked above Katie's.''

"Check Billy's?''

Clay thought his eyes would pop from his head. "Billy? She and Billy Jones together…?''

"At the garage. He was up all night putting the finishing touches on Delia's van. Said Red could take it back to her today."

"Red's gone back to D.C.?"

"To return the van." Jake shrugged. "But once she gets there, who knows what she'll do since a certain someone is too stubborn to tell her he loves her, and he does love her or he wouldn't have given up being sheriff."

Clay heaved a deep sigh. "I don't deserve to be sheriff, Jake. I knew Red was the senator's daughter and didn't turn her in."

"Which just proves you love her all the more. Saw Billy on my way here. Said if you were interested, he told Red not to take the van over twenty-five miles an hour because he recalibrated the fuel pump and it had to be broken in slowly. Something he made up to get her to drive slow, in case you wanted to catch up with her. Billy said that's all the time he's giving you, Clay. When Red gets back from D.C. he was making his move."

"Over my dead body." Clay kicked the trash can across the office, sending paper everywhere.

Jake put down his doughnut and neatly flicked powdered sugar from his uniform. "Red loves you. She wouldn't have staged that fight to get you to be sheriff, gotten ticked off when you thought she was going back to D.C., or gone looking for you 'cause she thought you might be in danger in the flood."

Clay sat down.

"What are you doing? I just told you the woman loves you. Why in tarnation are you sitting here? If you go after her it will help convince her you love her, too. And from what I heard transpired between you two last night it'll take *some* convincing."

Clay studied the wood floor. "But *why* does she love me?"

"What do you mean?"

He looked up. "What do I have to offer her? I'm nothing. No money, no power, no connections. Her father's a senator, and I don't even know who my father is."

"Albert's your daddy. If you don't take a chance and go after her, Clay, you'll spend the rest of your life a lonely old man who's missed out on a wonderful woman. It's your decision."

He had to take the chance. And he had to tell Red that he loved her. He owed her that no matter what. Clay held out his hand. "Let me have the keys to the cruiser."

Jake rocked back on his heels and stuffed his hands in his pockets. "Only a deputy and a sheriff can drive the cruiser, Clay."

Clay snapped the star from Jake's shirt. Looked at it and pinned it on his own chest. "Happy?"

"Tickled to my toes."

He shook Jake's hand. "Me, too."

AS CLAY DROVE, leaves tumbled to the ground, the sun turned yellows and reds to gold and rubies, a vee of geese winged overhead and clouds made soft pillows in the sky. This was all beautiful and terrific but it wouldn't count for squat if he couldn't convince Red to give him a second chance to make things right between them. He really did love her, was a jackass to not have pledged his love for her before now and he wanted a future with her. Hell, he wanted to marry her, *if* she would have him.

He rounded the next bend but there was no sign of her. Then up the next grade he spotted Delia's white and red van. He laid on the horn and waved, motioning for her to pull off to the side. She flashed him a very unladylike hand gesture that she sure couldn't have learned in any of those fancy schools she attended. She hunkered down in her seat and drove.

Did Jake mention groveling? From the looks of things, he'd have to do a lot of it.

She headed the van to the middle of the road and did some weaving back and forth so he couldn't pass her on the soft shoulders and cut her off.

She was going to get herself killed. The only thing saving her was the early hour—there were no other cars on the road. Damn the woman. She wasn't making this easy. Big surprise there.

Sharp's Cutoff was coming up. He'd take it, drive like a madman and intercept her at the next bend in the road. He wasn't waiting till she got back from D.C.

HOPE LOOKED IN HER rearview mirror and watched the cruiser take a turnoff. She had no idea what Clay wanted but she was in no mood to talk to him. Last night he'd made it quite clear the two of them were history. Could she pick men or what?

She reached into her pocket and pulled out the silver star Clay had given her that night at The Gray, the same one she'd tossed back to him, sliding it across the top of the cruiser, when he accused her of being a quitter. It had landed in the street and she'd gone back and searched in the mud till she found it. It was flattened like a bullfrog on the four-lane.

Wind whipped around inside the little van as she guided it back to the right side of the road. Even at twenty-five miles an hour she'd be back in D.C. by noon. As the van dogged its way around the next bend she ran her thumb over Sheriff etched in the middle. She'd return Delia's van, make amends by spreading her name on the Eastern Shore for catering jobs, take a few days to pack her things into her car, then head back to Paradise Creek. Clay Mitchell may not be *her* man, but Paradise Creek was her home.

She looked back to the road and saw red, yellow and blue flashing lights right in front of her, smack in the middle of the road and Clay waving his arms. She hit the brakes as Clay dove head-first to the side and the van smashed square into the middle of his cruiser.

"Holy cow." She jumped down from the van and ran toward Clay. He was laying face-up, wide-eyed, staring at the sky, dazed. "Are you all right? Say something?"

"I'm going to take your license and shred it."

"I don't have it, remember?" She pushed her hair from her face and glanced at the crash. "I think I killed your cruiser. Delia's not going to believe this."

He threw his arm over his face and groaned. "Your insurance company's the one who's not going to believe it."

Even lying on the side of the road in a pile of weeds, groaning, he looked unbelievably handsome. Handsome enough, tempting enough, to make her want to join him, *except he didn't love her.* "I thought you turned back."

"Surprise, surprise."

"What do you want?"

He stood, regained his footing, dusted himself off and glared down at her. "You."

She folded her arms. "Correct me if I'm wrong, but last night I distinctly remember you saying it wouldn't work. As in you and me."

"I...I..."

"You what? Don't love me? You made that incredibly clear."

"Of course I love you. I'll love you till the day I die. You're beautiful, smart, generous and sassy as hell and don't let me get away with anything. You're full of life and make everything exciting.''

He took a deep breath and swallowed. "What I don't get is why in the hell *you* love *me*."

He was serious. Very serious. Her heart squeezed tight. "You really don't know, do you?"

"I haven't a clue, Hope, I swear. It's not that I don't like who I am, but why would you? You were raised with the best of everything."

She wanted to hug him with all her might and chase away his doubts. But before she did that, she had to make him understand how she loved him and why. "You're right, I was raised with the best, and that's why I've fallen so completely in love with you. You *are* the best, Clay Mitchell. The best sheriff, the best lover, the best friend, the best man. You're honorable and steadfast and kind. A natural-born leader."

Then she threw her arms around him. "And you make me so happy. I'll never run away from you again. Love me, Clay, marry me and we'll live forever in paradise."

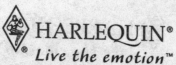

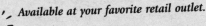
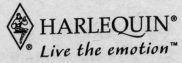

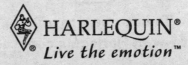

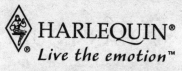

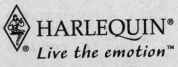